"Would you like to kiss me?" Amy asked

At Brendan's questioning look, Amy shrugged. "I was just curious. I mean, I know you were just trying to warm me up. But since I'm almost naked, and you're almost naked and we're lying in bed together, it's the next logical step, isn't it?"

Just the thought of kissing her, of pulling her body against his, pressing her breasts to his chest and cradling her hips in his brought a flood of desire rushing through Brendan. And it would be so easy. Just a pull here, a tug there and there would be nothing between him and Amy but skin.

So much for his self-control, Brendan thought, sitting up and raking his hands through his hair. Would he ever understand her? How could they go from discussing her background to... Brendan cursed softly as realization dawned. Amy had wanted to divert his questions about her past. Well, if she wanted a diversion...

Leaning back toward her, he braced his hands on either side of her head. "So, you want to know if I want to kiss you?" he asked innocently.

Amy's eyes went wide and she gave him a tiny nod.

"I think you deserve an answer, don't you?" he said, before bringing his mouth down on hers.

Dear Reader,

Planning and writing a trilogy is always a daunting experience. Throughout the planning of THE MIGHTY QUINNS, I often wondered if I'd finish. And now that I have, I'm sorry the miniseries is all over. Conor, Dylan and Brendan Quinn have been three of my most intriguing heroes. And when you spend months with men like these, it's a little hard to move on to someone else!

THE MIGHTY QUINNS concludes this month with Brendan's story. He's seen what's happened to his two older brothers and he's determined to avoid the same fate. This Quinn is *not* falling in love! Then he meets Amy Aldrich, a waitress in a waterfront bar, who is so much more than she appears to be. She moves into his life and soon, into his heart. And before he knows it, Brendan is the third Mighty Quinn to succumb to the love of a woman.

For those of you who aren't ready for this series to end, I have a surprise for you. In June 2002, a fourth Mighty Quinn book, *Reunited*, will hit the shelves as a single-title release. If you've been reading carefully, you might already know what's in store. So enjoy Brendan's story and watch for *Reunited* in June. And drop by my new Web site at www.katehoffmann.com for more information on all my books and future releases.

Enjoy,

Kate Hoffmann

Kate Hoffmann
THE MIGHTY QUINNS: BRENDAN

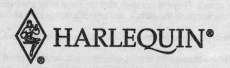

TORONTO • NEW YORK • LONDON
AMSTERDAM • PARIS • SYDNEY • HAMBURG
STOCKHOLM • ATHENS • TOKYO • MILAN • MADRID
PRAGUE • WARSAW • BUDAPEST • AUCKLAND

For my little sister, NeeNee

ISBN 0-373-25955-7

THE MIGHTY QUINNS: BRENDAN

This edition published by arrangement with Harlequin Books S.A.

® and TM are trademarks of the publisher. Trademarks indicated with ® are registered in the United States Patent and Trademark Office, the Canadian Trade Marks Office and in other countries.

Visit us at www.eHarlequin.com

Printed in U.S.A.

____Prologue____

THE MIDSUMMER HEAT shimmered off the pavement of Kilgore Street as Brendan Quinn slowly climbed the front steps of his house, a weatherbeaten two-story in the middle of the block. The screen door hung crookedly from its hinges and all the windows were thrown open allowing even the smallest hint of a breeze to ruffle the old lace curtains. He listened for his brothers and when he didn't hear any voices, he breathed a slow sigh of relief, then wiped a trickle of sweat from his cheek.

Though an occasional thunderstorm would provide a respite from the heat, the six Quinn brothers had taken to sleeping on the rickety back porch of the house, turning necessity into yet another adventure. Last night they'd even started a fire in the backyard and cooked hot dogs and marshmallows on sticks, just as if they were on a real vacation at the Grand Canyon or maybe the Rocky Mountains, rather than in the middle of a sweltering Boston summer.

There were no family vacations for the Quinns. Their father, Seamus, had been out to sea on his swordfishing boat for nearly a month. In a few days, he'd arrive back home and stay long enough to get drunk five or six times, gamble away most of the money he had made and reacquaint himself with his sons. Then he'd head out again.

Slowly, Brendan lowered himself onto the top step, wincing against the pain as he moved. He didn't want to go inside. After nearly a week of ninety degree days in the South Boston neighborhood, Brendan was sure it would be more pleasant walking into a blast furnace than into the Quinn house. Besides, he didn't want to face the inevitable questions—like how he got the black eye and the bloody nose and the cut lip.

If he was lucky, sixteen-year-old Conor would be at work at a nearby grocery store where he had a job as a bag boy. And Dylan, two years younger, would be washing cars with his buddy Tommy Flanagan over at Tommy's house.

But Brendan couldn't be bothered with work. There were too many adventures to be had in the summer, too many places to be seen to be tied down with a regular job. Just last week he'd taken the train all the way to New York City and back again, without paying, and the images of skyscrapers still swirled in his mind. The week before, he'd hopped a Greyhound bus for the exotic sounding destination of Nova Scotia, making it to the Canadian border before the driver realized he had a stowaway. And in a few weeks, he'd take a turn on his father's swordboat. But today, he'd stuck closer to home, wandering through the neighborhood for lack of anyplace better to go.

"Someday, I'll have enough money to travel the world," he murmured, staring down at the ragged toe of his tennis shoe. "And nothing will keep me here."

A few seconds later, his little brother Liam burst out

of the house, the screen door slamming behind him. He stopped cold at the sight of Brendan, his eyes growing wide. "What the hell happened to you?" he asked.

"Geez, Liam, don't you be swearing now. You're only nine years old and it isn't proper."

Liam spun on his heel and tore back into the house. "Con! Con! Come quick. Brendan's had the livin' crap beat out of him."

Brendan groaned at his little brother's colorful language. Though he, Conor and Dylan tried to maintain some level of discipline with the younger boys, the task was sometimes impossible. Liam reappeared at the door, followed closely by Conor who gave the boy a cuff on the head. "Stop your swearin', Liam Quinn, or I'll beat the livin' crap out of you."

His older brother stepped out onto the porch, his gaze fixed on Brendan's face. "Ya look like you've been run over by a truck, boyo."

Con sat down beside him, then began to poke and prod at the scrapes on Brendan's face. Besides the split lip and the sore ribs, Brendan felt pretty damn good, though he wasn't keen to dance a jig any time soon.

"Who did this to you?" Con asked.

"Angus Murphy," Brendan said. "He and a couple of his goons jumped me just a few blocks from here." Angus Murphy—all five feet six, two hundred pounds of him—was well-known to anyone living within a five block radius of Kilgore Street. As the designated neighborhood bully, he had it out for the Quinns. He'd tried to beat up Conor a few years back, but had lost badly. So he'd moved on to Dylan and got himself roundly pummeled. Brendan had known sooner or later his number would come up.

"I swear, Angus Murphy is the size of a small truck. When I first punched him, my fist just sank into that fat gut of his. Like punchin' a pillow and he didn't even blink. But then I got him a good puck in the gob and the fight was on. Surprised him that."

"Just tell me one thing, Bren," Dylan said. "Does he look worse than you?"

Brendan smiled up at his brother who'd just emerged from the house with a handful of ice cubes wrapped in an old dishtowel. Dylan handed the ice to Brendan then sat down on the other side of him. A few seconds later, the twins, Brian and Sean, appeared from the backyard, their clothes covered with dirt.

Brendan pressed the ice to his swollen lip. "He looked worse than me before the fight. That boy is as ugly as a mud fence." He grimaced. "God, I hate fighting."

In truth, Brendan had had his hands full with Angus. Though he didn't give anything away to him in height, Angus was at least seventy pounds heavier. But his weight made him slow on his feet and with every punch thrown, Brendan simply dodged and weaved, suffering a few glancing blows.

"I was winnin' for sure until I knocked Angus half-senseless." Brendan chuckled. "Then he fell on top of me. Like a big tree. And when he hit the ground, I felt the earth shake. I swear I did! Just like that giant, Fomor, in the story of Mighty Odran Quinn."

Liam's eyes brightened at the mention of one of the Mighty Quinns. Liam loved the stories. For as long as

Brendan could remember, the stories had been part of their lives. They'd started after his mother had walked out. At the time, Brendan hadn't made the connection, but as he got older he realized that Seamus Quinn's tall tales about their mighty Quinn ancestors were nothing but cautionary tales meant to warn his sons about the dangers of love.

After Fiona Quinn had walked out nearly eight years ago, life had never been the same. Though Con and Dylan had memories of her, Brendan had only been four years old. He had vague images of a dark-haired woman who sang songs and made him cookies. He remembered a birthday cake in the shape of a car. And a beautiful necklace she always wore. But beyond that, Brendan had relied on his older brothers for a picture of his mother for there were no mementos of her left in the house.

She was beautiful and affectionate and understanding, all the best qualities magnified a hundred times in their imaginations. Alone at night, he and Con and Dylan used to wonder aloud whether she might still be alive, whether she had miraculously walked away from the auto accident that his father insisted had claimed her life. Brendan liked to believe that she had amnesia and that she was living another life with a new family and that someday she would suddenly remember the boys she'd left behind.

"God, I hate fightin'," Brendan repeated. "I mean, what good does it do? Angus will still be a bully. He'll just move on to someone else." He glanced at the twins. "You're next, you know."

"Some goms only respond to the sting of a fist or the taste of blood on their lip," Conor said.

"If you ask me," Dylan said, "someone ought to whack that boy over the head once or twice with a nice thick plank, maybe jangle his brain a bit."

"You were like Dermot," Liam said, his eyes filled with awe. "Remember Dermot Quinn? How he fought off all those boys from the village."

Brendan reached out and ruffled his little brother's hair. "I'm not sure I do remember Dermot," he said. "Why don't you tell me, Liam. Maybe it will make me feel a little better."

His little brother drew a deep breath and began. "Some boys who were jealous of Dermot decided to drown him. They pretended they were swimming and—"

"That's not where it starts," Sean insisted. "It starts when Dermot catches the deer."

Brian shook his head. "No, it starts when Dermot is born inside the giant oak tree."

Liam leaned over and braced his elbows on Brendan's leg. "You tell it," he pleaded. "You do it best."

Brendan took a deep breath. "Well, Dermot Quinn was raised in the forest by two strong and wise women, one a Druidess and the other a warrior. They raised him after his father was killed by an evil chieftain. Living all that time in the forest, Dermot became a fine hunter. One day, he was walking with the two women and they spotted a herd of deer. 'I would love to have venison for dinner tonight,' the Druidess said. But none of them had brought along a weapon."

Liam sat up and continued. "'I can catch that deer

for you,' Dermot cried. And he did. He ran after the herd and he captured a huge buck with his bare hands and wrestled it to the ground."

"That he did," Brendan said. "And then, the two women told Dermot since he was now a great hunter, he must learn to become a great warrior. So they sent him on a long journey to search for a teacher." Brendan glanced over at Conor who nodded and continued the story, drawing Liam's attention away from Brendan's bleeding nose.

"One day, Dermot passed a group of boys playing a game," Conor said. "They invited him to play, but they made him play by himself against five of the boys. Dermot won the game. The next day, they put ten boys against him and still he won. And the next day, all the boys in the village played and he won again. The boys were embarrassed and complained to the chieftain. A vengeful and powerful man, the chieftain told the boys that if they didn't like Dermot, they must kill him.

"So the next day, they decided to invite Dermot to swim with them in the lake. They ganged up on him and tried to drown him, but Dermot was strong and in the end, he drowned nine of the boys defending himself. When the chieftain heard this, he suspected that Dermot was the son of his old enemy, a man he murdered many years before. He set out to find Dermot and deal him the same fate."

"But Dermot didn't want to fight," Brendan said. "He was a peaceful person. So he decided to become a poet, for poets were held in very high esteem in Ireland. The evil chieftain would be unable to harm him if he were a poet. Dermot returned to the forest and found a teacher who lived near a great river. His name was Finney and every day they would talk as Finney fished in the river, hoping to catch a magic salmon who lived in the shallow water."

"The fish was charmed," Liam said. "And whoever ate the fish would have—have—"

"Knowledge of all things," Brendan completed. "Finney was keen to catch this fish. For years he fished and Dermot patiently watched him and one day Finney finally caught the fish. He gave it to Dermot to cook for him, but he warned him that he must not taste the fish for it held powerful magic. Dermot did as he was told but as the fish cooked in a tasty stew, a drop of the stew splashed on Dermot's thumb. He cried out and put his thumb in his mouth to cool the pain."

"So he did taste the fish," Liam said.

"That he did," Brendan replied. "And when he served the fish to Finney, he admitted as much. 'Then you must eat the salmon,' his teacher said. 'And from this fish you will receive a gift so precious to poets— the gift of great words. And after that, Dermot's poetry became the most beloved in all of Ireland."

"Are you going to fight Angus again?" Liam asked.

"Nope," Brendan replied. "I don't like fighting. I think I'm going to become a poet like Dermot Quinn. For Dermot proved that words can be as mighty as weapons."

As Brendan sat on the front porch of the house on Kilgore Street, he thought about the Mighty Quinns, all those ancestors that had come before, all those Quinns who'd made something of themselves. He wasn't sure how he knew, but Brendan was certain that something special was waiting for him out in the world. But it wouldn't come to him if he stayed here. He'd need to go find it.

1

Brendan Quinn sat in a dark corner of the Longliner Tap, nursing a warm beer and watching the patrons wallow in their Friday night rituals. The Longliner was a popular spot for commercial fishermen, their families and their friends, located on the rough and tumble waterfront of Gloucester, Massachusetts, homebase to the North Atlantic swordfishing fleet.

His own home, *The Mighty Quinn*, was tied up at a dock just a few hundred yards from the bar. Though the early December cold had set in, his father's old swordboat was tight and cozy, providing a perfect spot for him to tie up the loose ends on his latest book.

He'd come to the Longliner to talk just once more to those family members and friends of the fishermen he'd profiled, hoping to find a new slant to his book about the dangers and adventures the men faced while making a living on the open ocean. He'd interviewed six different people that night, scribbling notes on scraps of paper in between conversations, plying his subjects with free beer to loosen their tongues.

Now that he'd finished, he just wanted to relax and absorb the atmosphere. The majority of the Gloucester fishermen who frequented the Longliner had already headed south for the season, but there were a few stragglers who hadn't picked up a job on a boat for the winter, men used to working hard and playing even harder. And then there were the girlfriends and wives of those who were gone. They came to the bar to share their loneliness with other women who understood what they went through year after year.

Brendan's gaze fastened on a petite blond waitress who wove through the crowd, a tray of beers held high over her head. Throughout the night, his gaze had come back to her again and again. There was something about her that wasn't quite right, something that didn't fit. Though she wore the standard costume—a canvas apron, impossibly tight jeans and a low-cut T-shirt that looked like it might have been painted on—she still didn't seem to fit.

It wasn't the hair, bleached a honey-blond, or the makeup, the dark eyes and bright red lips. Or even the three earrings she wore in each ear. He watched her for a long moment as she served drinks to a table of rowdy men. It was the way she moved. So unlike the other waitresses, with their hips swinging and breasts thrown out in obvious invitation. She was graceful, refined, not at all provocative. She seemed to glide across the floor almost like a dancer. The arch in her long neck and the turn of her arm added to the illusion that she wasn't serving beers to a bunch of waterfront rats but floating across the stage with Baryshnikov.

She turned away from the table and Brendan raised his hand, curious enough about her to order another beer. But just as he caught her eye and she moved toward him, one of the wharf rats at the table grabbed her from behind and dragged her into his lap. In an instant, his paws were all over her.

As the tawdry scene unfolded, Brendan groaned inwardly. The situation was fast getting out of control and no one else seemed overly concerned. He knew of only one solution. "God, I hate fighting," he muttered. He shoved his chair back and stalked across the bar to stand beside the table. "Take your hands off the lady," he ordered, his fists clenched at his side, his instincts sharp.

The drunken lout looked up at him and gave him a sneer. "What did you say, pretty boy?"

"I said, take your hands off the lady."

The waitress reached out and touched his arm. He looked down at her and was immediately struck by how young she was. For some reason, he'd expected a face lined by years of hard work and hard living. But instead he found a complexion so fresh, so perfect, that he was tempted to reach out and touch her to see if she was real.

"I can handle this," she said. "You don't need to get involved. I'm very good with conflict resolution and interpersonal communications. I took a seminar once."

Her voice was low and throaty, the sound like whiskey on a cold night, drawing him in closer, warming his blood. Brendan reached down and took her hand, then pulled her to her feet. "Go on," he said. "I'll take care of this."

This time she clutched his jacket sleeve with her fingers. Her touch sent a current shooting up his arm. "No, really. I can take care of this. There's no need to fight. Violence never solves anything." She stared up at him with eyes so blue it hurt to look at them. "Please," she pleaded.

Brendan wasn't sure what to do. It wasn't in his nature to just walk away from a woman in need. Especially not after being raised listening to all those Mighty Quinn tales of heroic deeds and chivalrous behavior. He glanced over to find the rest of the patrons silently watching, holding their collective breaths to see whether he'd turn tail or stay and fight. And in that brief instant, the decision was made for him.

When he turned back around to the waitress, he saw a flicker of movement in the corner of his eye. The beer bottle came flying at his head and Brendan dodged. It whizzed past his ear and hit one of the drunks at the table, catching him on the temple before it fell to the floor and shattered. After that, all hell broke loose.

The waitress grabbed a plastic pitcher of beer and poured it over her attacker's head then began to beat him with the pitcher. Brendan dodged another bottle and then a fist before catching a glancing blow to his chin. Determined to retreat before either one of them got seriously injured, he grabbed the waitress's arm and dragged her away from the nucleus of the brawl. But she slipped from his grasp and jumped on the back of one of the drunks, boxing his ears with her fists.

Brendan had to admire the patrons of the Longliner Tap. They chose sides and they did it quickly, then threw themselves into the middle of an escalating melee, either with their fists or with verbal encouragement.

"God, I hate fighting," he muttered. He was tempted to turn and walk away. But he couldn't just leave the waitress in the middle of it all. He glanced over at her as she wielded a tray like some Ninja weapon. She whacked one drunk across the head then stomped on the instep of another when he came to the aid of his injured friend.

No one seemed to be concerned for her safety. Those patrons not involved in the fight were cheering her on. The rest of the waitresses had perched on the bar to get a better view of the fight. One bartender was on the phone, probably summoning the local constables, and the other had pulled out a baseball bat and was waving it in a threatening manner. But as the fight escalated, Brendan wondered whether the police would get there in time.

When a burly fisherman grabbed the waitress from behind and picked her up off her feet, Brendan took a step forward. She kicked the guy in the kneecap with the heel of her boot, then screamed for help. Although a voice in his head told him to mind his own business, Brendan knew he was about to end up right back in the middle of the mess.

The original lout stood in the midst of the brawl. Brendan saw him step up to the waitress, shout something at her, then draw his hand back to slap her. Though he wasn't anxious to play white knight, Brendan couldn't seem to help himself. Hitting a woman was unacceptable. He stepped between the man and the waitress. "Don't even think about it," Brendan warned.

"You gonna stop me?" the man growled. "You and what army?"

Brendan cursed softly. God, he *hated* fighting. But sometimes, a guy just couldn't avoid it. "No army," he said, turning away. "Just me." Brendan drew his fist back, then launched a roundhouse punch that caught the guy on the nose. He howled in pain as blood spurted from his nose.

Then Brendan turned around to the hulk who was holding the waitress. A left cross and a punch to the kidney was enough for the guy to let her go. Brendan grabbed her arm, but to his shock, she pulled away from him.

"Let me go!" she cried.

He grabbed her again. "Don't make me carry you out of here," he warned. "Because, I'm not going to do it." This was how it all began—for Conor and then for Dylan. Not the fight, but the rescue. This was exactly how they ended up trapped by a woman's charms and madly in love. They each had saved a damsel in distress and their lives were never the same again. The hell if he was going to make *that* mistake.

"I'm not leaving! I can take care of myself!" With a curse, she jammed her heel onto *his* instep.

Pain shot up his leg. He ground his teeth and tried desperately to hold his tongue. "Listen," he said, his voice deceptively calm. "I'm not going to tell you again." He grabbed her arm more firmly this time and dragged her toward the door.

"Help!" she screamed. "Help me!"

"I'm not going to do it," Brendan muttered. "I'm not going to throw you over my shoulder and carry you out of here. If I do, it'll be the end of my life as I know it."

"Someone, please. He's kidnapping me!"

"Aw, hell." Brendan stopped, bent over, grabbed her around the legs then hoisted her over his shoulder and strode to the door. A few of the patrons not involved in the fight cheered and some threw popcorn like rice at a wedding. With a tight smile, Brendan waved at them then yanked the door open and walked outside into the cold night.

When he got outside, he looked up and down the dark street. The sound of sirens approaching told him he'd gotten out of the bar just in time. Considering he'd instigated the fight, it might be best to avoid the authorities.

"Put me down," the waitress said, wriggling and kicking.

"Not yet," Brendan replied as he started across the street. He headed toward the docks and when they were far enough from the bar to escape notice, he bent over and set the girl on her feet. But he didn't let go right away. "You aren't going to run back inside, are you? Because I'd hate to think that I almost killed myself saving your pretty little backside only to have you jump right back into the fight."

"The cops are here," she murmured. "I'm not going back inside."

Satisfied, Brendan unwrapped his arms from around her legs and straightened. They stood under a bright streetlamp near the end of the pier. Brendan's gaze skimmed over her features. Despite the unflattering glare, he was even more astounded by her beauty. She didn't have the cool, sophisticated features of Olivia, Conor's wife. Or the cute, natural beauty of Dylan's Meggie. This girl had a look that was wild and unpredictable, edgy and rebellious, as if she didn't care what people thought of her.

She obviously didn't care what *he* thought of her. The glare she sent his way bordered on murderous. "If you're expecting me to thank you, I wouldn't hold my breath." She rubbed her arms and shivered, her chin tipped up defiantly.

The temperature was below freezing and all she wore was a skimpy T-shirt. Brendan slipped out of his jacket and draped it around her shoulders. "My boat's just down the dock here," he said. "Why don't you come with me and I'll make us some coffee. The cops should be gone in about a half hour and then you can go back."

She eyed him suspiciously. "Why should I go with you? How do I know you're not exactly like the guy you punched out, all paws and no brain?"

"Fine," Brendan said. "Stand out here in the cold." He turned on his heel and started down the dock. He smiled as he heard footsteps behind him.

"Wait!" she called.

Brendan slowed his steps until she joined him. When they reached his boat, he held her hand as she stepped up on an overturned crate and jumped lightly to the deck. Her fingers felt small and delicate in his hand and he held on for a bit longer than necessary.

The lights inside *The Mighty Quinn* burned brightly. When he opened the hatch and showed her through the companionway, she sighed softly. "I didn't take you for a fisherman," she said.

"I'm not," Brendan replied, following her down the steps into the main cabin. "My father was. When he retired, I started living on the boat. I've gradually restored it, changed a few things around, opened up the galley. It makes a nice place to live, especially in the summer."

She rubbed her arms again, this time through the soft leather of his jacket. "In the winter, too," she said as she turned to face him.

Brendan's gaze skimmed her features and stopped at a red welt on her cheekbone. He reached out and touched her there, realizing his mistake the moment he made it. A current of attraction, as strong as an electrical shock, shot through him as his fingertips made contact with impossibly soft skin. "You're hurt," he murmured.

Her gaze locked with his, her blue eyes wide and wary. She reached up and covered his fingers with hers. "I am?"

He nodded. The urge to kiss her was strong and undeniable, even though every shred of common sense told him that it was completely inappropriate. They'd known each other ten minutes at the most. Hell, he didn't even know her name, yet here he was, tempted to sweep her into his embrace and taste her mouth! Brendan swallowed hard then realized exactly what was happening.

This was a self-fulfilling prophecy! He'd carried her out of the bar and now he could expect to fall head-over-heels in love with her...just like Conor...just like Dylan. Well, it wasn't going to happen. He liked his life exactly the way it was—free and unencumbered. Brendan drew his hand away. "I'll get you some ice," he muttered. He motioned to the table in the corner of the cabin. "Sit. It'll just take a second."

She did as she was told, sliding into a spot at the table then playing distractedly with a pencil she found there. He reached over and moved his laptop computer out of the way then straightened a stack of manuscript pages, tucking them beneath a file folder.

"So, if you're not a fisherman, what do you do?"

"I'm a writer," Brendan said grabbing a handful of ice from the small fridge in the galley. He wrapped it in a cotton towel then sat down next to her and gently pressed it to the red mark on her face. Without thinking, he brushed a strand of hair from her eyes and tucked it behind her ear. Then he realized how intimate the action seemed.

"I should go," she said, scrambling out of her place and putting a few feet of space between them.

At first, he thought he'd frightened her. But then he noticed the flicker of attraction in her eyes, the way her gaze flitted from his face to his body and back again. He wondered if he'd leaned forward and kissed her would she have drawn away or would she have responded?

She slipped out of his jacket and set it on the table beside him. "The cops have probably cleared out the rowdies by now and I'm working for tips. People are going to want their drinks and they're paying me to fetch them."

She turned toward the hatch, but Brendan grabbed her arm. He picked up his jacket and held it out to her. "Take this. It's cold outside."

She shook her head, her pale hair tumbling around her face. "No, I'm fine." She hesitated then gave him a quick smile, the only smile she'd cast his way since they'd met. "Thanks. For the jacket. And for coming to my rescue."

With that she was gone, disappearing into the cold December night and returning to a world to which she didn't seem to belong. Brendan almost went after her, curious to know her name and her story, wondering what had brought her to work at the Longliner. Was she the girlfriend of a fisherman? Had she grown up in Gloucester? And why did her eyes remind him of the sky on a perfect spring day?

He backed away from the hatch and shook his head. He'd had his doubts about carrying her out of the bar. That had been his first mistake. It would be stupid to compound the error by going after her. She was out of his life, no harm, no foul. He should be happy he'd gotten away so cleanly.

Yet as he made himself a pot of coffee and settled down to work at his laptop computer, Brendan's thoughts returned to her again and again, to that winsome smile and that spark of mischief in her eyes. To the curious air of mystery that seemed to surround her. And to the way he felt the instant he touched her, as if they'd made some strange, magnetic connection.

Brendan shook his head and refocussed on his work. She was gone and he was better off for it. Though Conor and Dylan had fallen into lifelong commitment and everlasting love, Brendan was pragmatic enough to know that he wasn't meant to do the same. His work required the freedom to come and go at will and he had to protect that freedom at all costs.

Even if it meant walking away from the most intriguing woman he'd met in years.

"YOU CAN'T FIRE ME! It wasn't my fault."

Amelia Aldrich Sloane stood outside the Longliner, staring up at the second floor above the bar. The owner of the bar was silhouetted in the window of her tiny room. He tossed out a garbage bag stuffed with her belongings and it landed with a "whoof" at her feet.

"I warned you the last time," he said, leaning out the window. "One more fight and you were through. Do you know how much damage you caused?"

"It's not my fault," Amy repeated.

"The hell it isn't," he shouted back.

"How is it my fault?" she demanded.

"You're too damn pretty," he said tossing her suitcase out the window. "You're like catnip to a bunch of tomcats. Men can't seem to keep their hands off you and that starts fights. And fights cost me money, sweetheart. Much more than you're worth as a waitress."

"But I need this job," Amy cried, running to grab her suitcase as it hit the ground and burst open.

"I hear Buddy's House of Crabs is hiring. Get a job there." With that he slammed the window shut, leaving Amy to stand on the silent street. She cursed softly then grabbed her jacket from the heap and slipped it on. "Well, I wanted adventure in my life," she muttered, gathering her things. "I guess I should be careful what I wish for."

It was half past two in the morning and she'd just lost her room and her job all in one fell swoop. She should have known something was wrong when she had returned to the bar and the other waitresses had refused to talk to her. The owner had been summoned by the police and when he finally got the full story, he'd pulled Amy aside and told her to clear out.

At first, she thought he was kidding. But when he climbed the stairs to her room and started tossing her belongings out onto the street, she had no choice. She'd raced outside to collect what she could before the bar patrons stumbling home after closing time were able to grab a souvenir or two. As it was, they all got a nice round of chuckles from her predicament.

"Now what am I supposed to do?" she murmured. Working at the Longliner had been the perfect setup. She needed to stay below the radar and seeing as she worked for tips only, the owner had no need for proof of her identity or her social security number. But the wandering hands of a customer and her rather indignant response had put an end to what she'd hoped would be a long-term job.

She hadn't had much of a plan when she'd left her life back in Boston, only that she was determined to get as far away from her old life as possible—away from her dictatorial father and her socialite mother, away from their powerful influence over her life. And most of all, far away from her scheming fiancé, the man who'd grown to love the Aldrich money more than he loved Amy.

Her life had been planned for her from the moment she was born, the only child of Avery Aldrich Sloane and his beautiful wife Dinah. And for most of her life, she'd dutifully followed the plan. But then one day, just a week before her big society wedding to Craig Atkinson Talbot, she'd come to the realization that if she stayed, she would never really live her own life.

She had been on the run for nearly six months, lucky enough to keep just one step ahead of the private detectives her father had hired. She'd lived in Salem, in Worcester and in Cambridge, picking up odd waitressing jobs and calling on old friends to put her up on their sofas. She figured if she could just keep out of sight for another six months, then she was in the clear. The trust fund her grandmother had set up for her would be all hers, no strings attached. The day she turned twenty-six years old, she'd become a comfortably wealthy woman, a woman free to experience all the things she'd missed in life, free to search for adventure and excitement.

As she arranged her belongings neatly on a bench in front of the bait shop, she thought about what the money would mean. She'd always rejected her parents' obsession with financial matters, thinking their avaricious nature somehow unseemly. But since she'd been trying to live on her own, Amy had realized that money, at least a small amount of it, came in pretty handy.

Though she'd been brought up in the lap of luxury, Amy had always wanted to test her parents' boundaries. She'd argued for public school, but was forced to attend an exclusive private prep school. When she'd insisted on a public university, a big college where she could get lost in the crowd, her parents gave her a choice of Sarah Lawrence or Vassar. That time she won a small victory, choosing Columbia University in New York.

It was at graduate school at Columbia where she'd met her fiancé, a wonderful man from a good Boston family who was studying law, hoping to open a community law office. When she'd first introduced him to her parents, they'd been pleased with his family connections but worried over his career prospects. He was the perfect man for her next rebellious step.

But that soon changed once Craig fell under the spell of her father's money and influence. It wasn't long before he was working for Aldrich Industries as a corporate lawyer. A few months before their wedding, he was promoted to Executive Corporate Counsel, a powerful position that came with a six-figure salary and stock options. It was then that Amy realized his dream of a community law office had been put aside and that the man she'd fallen in love with was not the man she was about to marry.

So she ran. Just a week before she was scheduled to walk down the aisle, she packed a bag in the middle of the night, drove her car to the train station and hopped the last train out of town. She'd cleaned out her checking account the day before, giving her enough cash to live on for three months. That cash was long gone.

Amy reached into her pocket and withdrew a wad of bills she'd collected as tips. By the light from the streetlamp, she began to count it, wondering if she'd have enough for a room for the night. She glanced up at the sound of footsteps, quickly hiding the money in her jacket pocket. But then she recognized the man who approached. It was the guy who'd started the fight in the bar, the man responsible for her predicament.

It was as if he appeared from nowhere again to rescue her, her hero with the dark windblown hair and the chiseled features. Amy swallowed hard. A shiver of attraction raced through her but she refused to acknowledge it. She was cold. She'd been sitting outside for fifteen minutes and she was simply cold, that's what caused the shiver. "What are you doing here?" she asked when he stopped in front of the bench.

"I was just taking a walk to clear my head," he said. "What are you doing sitting out here? You shouldn't be here all alone. Are you waiting for a ride home?"

"Actually, that was home," she said, pointing back to the Longliner. "I lived above the bar...until about fifteen minutes ago. Until you got me booted out of my job and my place to stay."

"Me?"

"You heard me," Amy said. "Because of you, I lost my job and my place to stay, not to mention two decent, though incredibly greasy, meals a day. I told you I could take care of that guy."

"He had his hands all over you."

Amy laughed softly. "You don't hang out much at the Longliner, do you? That's par for the course. Besides, a little grope here and there makes the tips better. I know my own limits and I know how to enforce them."

He shook his head. "The owner couldn't have fired you just because of one fight—a fight that really wasn't your fault. Let me go talk to him. I'll—"

"This was my third fight, if you must know. I guess he was getting a little sick of paying for shattered glasses and broken tables."

He sat down next to her, bracing his elbows on his knees. "You must have friends or family you could call."

Amy shook her head, warmed by his concern. "No. My family lives on the west coast," she lied. "Besides, we don't talk much. And I haven't been here long enough to make friends."

"Well, where are you going to go?"

Amy shrugged. "I don't know. I'll figure out something."

He cursed beneath his breath. "I suppose you don't have money for a motel room?"

She heard the concern in his voice, caught the trace of guilt in his expression. He did believe this was his responsibility, even though Amy knew it really wasn't. She reached in her jacket pocket and pulled out the cash she'd made on tips—barely thirty dollars. "It's your fault, you know. I was handling the problem. If you wouldn't have butted in, I could have stopped the fight. But as soon as you pulled me out of there, all hell broke loose."

"If you had stayed, you would have gotten hurt," he said.

"We'll never know, will we."

They sat on the bench for a long time, staring out at the harbor, their breath clouding in front of their faces. Then he stood up and grabbed the garbage bag and her leather suitcase. "Come on, then," he muttered.

Amy stood up and snatched the bag from his hand. "Come on where?"

"You can stay with me. There's a crew cabin on my boat. It's clean and warm. You can spend the night and tomorrow you can find a new job and a new place to live."

Amy gasped, completely taken aback by his offer.

She'd expected a few extra dollars for a motel room, maybe an offer of a ride. "Stay with you? I don't even know your name. How do I know you're not some psychopathic serial killer?"

"I guess you don't," he said.

"What's your name?"

"Brendan Quinn," he replied. "What's yours?"

"Amy Aldrich." She stared at him for a long moment. "Brendan Quinn. I suppose that doesn't sound like a serial killer's name."

"I told you, I'm a writer."

She motioned him closer. Reaching out, she touched his chin and tipped his head up to the light. "You look like you have an honest face. I'm very intuitive and I'm sure I'll be safe with you."

"I'm sure you will," Brendan replied. He held out his hand and she hesitantly placed her fingers in his. "It's nice to meet you, Amy Aldrich."

They started off back down the dock, Amy glancing over at him every now and then. He really was quite handsome. She'd noticed that the moment he'd walked up to her in the bar. His dark hair was just a bit too long, brushing the collar of his leather jacket, and his face was covered with the dark stubble of a day-old beard. But it was his eyes that captured her attention. They were an odd mixture of green and gold, not exactly hazel, something much more intriguing.

When they reached his boat, he tossed her belongings onboard then helped her on deck. She lugged her suitcase toward the hatch and then dragged it down the steps. As she took in the cozy interior, she sighed in relief. Although she'd be sleeping in a strange place,

Amy somehow knew that she'd be safe here. In truth, this would be the perfect spot to stay for the next few months.

"Can I make you anything to eat?" he asked.

Amy nodded, looking around the cabin, searching the place for more clues about the man she was entrusting with her safety. He lived comfortably. Though the interior of the cabin wasn't luxurious, it was functional. And tidy. The shelves of books and the laptop computer proved his claim to be a writer.

"Where do I stay?" she asked.

He pointed forward. "First door on your right. There should be an empty bunk."

"Where's the head?" she asked.

He paused and looked at her. "You know boats?"

Amy shrugged and started forward. "My dad had a small boat." She stepped inside the crew cabin. In truth, her father had a huge boat, a yacht on which she and her mother had spent summer vacations cruising the Mediterranean while her father stayed in Boston. She tossed her things on one of the lower berths, then rummaged through a bag for clean clothes. What she wore smelled of smoke and stale beer.

When she emerged from the bathroom with a freshly scrubbed face and clean clothes, she found him waiting for her at the table. She sat down next to him and picked up the glass of milk he'd poured for her then took a slow sip. "I really appreciate this," she said, setting the milk down and licking her upper lip.

"No problem," he murmured, his gaze fixed for a moment on her mouth.

To distract his attention, she took a bite of the ham

sandwich he'd prepared. She'd been so used to eating bar food for every meal that a simple ham sandwich tasted like gourmet fare. "Why did you jump into the middle of that fight?" Amy asked. "I was in a roomful of men and you were the only one who came to my aid. Why was that?"

"I don't know," Brendan said. "You just looked like you needed me."

"The same way I needed you outside the bar?" Amy asked.

"Yeah, maybe." Brendan chuckled.

"But why?"

He shrugged. "When I was a kid my Da used to tell us stories about our ancestors. The Mighty Quinns. They were always the heroes, brave and strong, chivalrous. I guess the stories stuck."

Amy smiled, then leaned over and gave him a quick kiss on the cheek. "I'm glad they did," she murmured. She picked up her sandwich and her milk and pushed away from the table. "I'll see you in the morning."

When she reached the safety of her cabin, Amy shut the door behind her and leaned back against it, clutching the milk and her ham sandwich to her chest. She smiled, then took a bite of the sandwich. It was nice to have a hero, someone who cared more about her than the Aldrich money. But how far would this stranger— would Brendan Quinn—go to help her?

Amy sighed. There was an even bigger question out there. How long would she be able to resist such a handsome and charming protector?

2

HE WASN'T completely asleep when he heard the knock on the door of his cabin. At first, Brendan thought it was his imagination, part of a dream he had briefly slipped into before drifting off. But the knock came again and he pushed up on his elbow and rubbed his eyes. There could be only one person on the other side and considering his earlier reaction to Amy Aldrich, Brendan wasn't sure that a late-night visit was in his best interest. He rolled over and closed his eyes.

She knocked again, this time more insistently. With a soft curse, he reached out and turned on the light beside his berth. "Come in," he called.

The door opened a crack and Amy peered inside. "I'm sorry to wake you," she said in a low whisper. "But my cabin is freezing. Do you have another blanket?"

Brendan groaned inwardly. He wasn't really set up for guests on *The Mighty Quinn*. When one of his brothers stayed overnight, they usually didn't require much in terms of amenities. The only other blanket he had was the down comforter that he was sleeping beneath and if he gave that up, he wouldn't be able to sleep at all. "Put on another layer of clothes," he suggested.

She opened the door wider and in the dim light, he could see that she'd already done that. She looked like a refugee from some bizarre slumber party, layers of clothing and pajamas turning her pretty figure into one that resembled the Pillsbury Doughboy. Topping it all off, she wore a hooded sweatshirt with the hood tied tightly around her face. He could hear her teeth chattering from across the room. If he had any worries about his attraction to her, they ended with the red wool gloves she wore on her hands and the fuzzy slippers on her feet.

"I'm going to die of hypothermia," Amy said. "And it's going to be all your fault."

Brendan groaned and flopped back on the bed, his arm over his eyes. "Why is it that everything bad that happens to you is my fault?"

She walked across his cabin and sat down on the edge of his berth, tugging the edge of down comforter over her shoulders. "Because it is," she murmured. "You could give me this blanket."

Though Amy didn't look as sexy as she potentially could, the notion of her sitting on his berth in the middle of the night was a bit disconcerting for him. He'd never brought a woman home to *The Mighty Quinn* before. The boat was his own personal space and Brendan had always felt that inviting someone here, especially for the purposes of pleasure, would be a violation of his privacy. Sure, Olivia had been on his boat and so had Meggie. Olivia had even slept in his bed—with Conor. And now that Amy Aldrich was here, he wasn't even sure why he was so concerned. She was simply a guest, after all, not a lover.

But that changed the instant Amy lay down beside him. Pulling the down comforter over top of her and wriggling up against him, she settled in. He became acutely aware that he wasn't wearing anything but the comforter and an uneasy smile, not that she could tell through the five layers of clothes she wore. "What the hell are you doing?" Brendan asked.

"I'm just going to lie here until I warm up. Then I'll go back to my cabin," she murmured. "You know, it's really not the cold. It's the damp. It just goes right to the bone."

Brendan sat up and jammed the coverlet between their bodies. He didn't mean to act like a prude, but this was totally unacceptable. "You're not going to sleep in here," he said. "This is my cabin."

Amy turned over. "What's the big deal? It's not like anything is going to happen. I'm just trying to get warm."

"Go back to your own cabin, Amy," he said through clenched teeth.

"No," she replied, tugging the comforter more tightly around her. "I want to stay here." She watched him warily. "You don't have to worry. I'm not going to attack you while you sleep. I'm not even attracted to you. You're just a warm body." With a frustrated sigh, she pulled one of the pillows from beneath his head. "You do have a huge ego. As if I couldn't resist you. Please. You're not that cute." She laughed, then turned her back to him.

Well, he had his answer. If he thought there was even a flicker of attraction between them, he now knew it was strictly one-sided. She had no reservations about spending the night in his bed. Never mind that he was naked and in a state of tightly checked arousal. All she wanted was a warm place to sleep and he could provide that for her. But at what cost?

Brendan stared at her long and hard, then reached out and impatiently flicked a strand of her silken hair off of his pillow. "You stay on your side of the berth and I'll stay on mine," he warned. "Or you'll be sleeping on the floor."

"All right," she murmured, snuggling more deeply beneath the comforter.

But the barrier between them was very thin indeed. His berth was barely bigger than a twin-size bed and even jammed up against the wall, her backside came dangerously close to his lap. Brendan lay frozen in place, afraid to move, almost afraid to breathe.

Though it had been a long time since he'd slept with a woman, he'd never expected his next time to be like this. Sharing a bed with a woman usually meant a night of passion and excitement, culminating in an exquisite release. Instead, he was here with Nanook of the North, whose only interest in him was in how much body heat he might provide.

Brendan wasn't sure how long he lay like that, only that it was long after Amy had fallen asleep. She'd managed to wiggle up against him until his body cradled hers, until her hair tickled his face and her slow, even breathing was the only sound in the cabin. He tried to sleep, but every time he closed his eyes, unbidden fantasies swirled in his head. He imagined himself undressing her, tossing aside all those layers of clothes and pulling her body against his, skin meeting skin, the exchange of heat tantalizing and exciting, not a matter of practicality at all.

A cramp clutched at his leg and he groaned softly. The only way to stretch was to throw his leg over her hip. He did and the pain immediately eased. But a moment later, he realized what the action had cost him. He was now fully pressed against her backside and unable to quell a flood of arousal. With a low curse, Brendan backed away, but there was no more room on his side of the bed.

There was only one thing to do and the mere thought of it irritated him to no end. He scrambled over top of her and jumped out of the berth then snatched up a pair of jeans from a nearby chair and tugged them on.

He stood in the cabin and stared down at his guest, sleeping so peacefully, her body tucked into *his* bed. Any thought of sleep would be impossible as long as she was here. He considered carrying her back to her own cabin, but wasn't prepared for the protest that would certainly ensue. Instead, Brendan slipped out the door, walked into Amy's cabin and crawled beneath the rough wool blankets of her berth. The crew berths weren't really meant for comfort. They made efficient use of a small amount of space, allowing no room to stretch out, especially for anyone over six feet tall.

Brendan folded his hands over his chest and stared up at the bottom of the bunk above him. What in the world had ever possessed him to invite her to spend the night? From the very start, he knew she was trouble. She said whatever was on her mind, even if it was insulting. She acted as if he was the cause of all of her troubles, dishing up the guilt until he had no choice but to respond. And then she had the audacity to crawl into bed with him as if her behavior wasn't at all out of the ordinary!

Amy Aldrich definitely wasn't like any other woman he'd ever met before. She lived her life by a whole different set of rules and standards. Or maybe it was the complete lack of rules in her life that made her different. Either way, Brendan found himself completely intrigued, captivated by her beauty but even more caught by the woman behind that luminous skin and those tantalizing blue eyes.

Tomorrow he'd get up early and find a place for her to stay. Even if he had to pay for a week or two at some local motel, it would be well worth the price. Amy Aldrich had swept into his life and upset the balance he worked so hard to achieve. If he let her stay, there was no telling what might happen. He might completely lose his mind and fall in love, just like Conor and Dylan had done with such startling speed.

No, this was not going to result in the fall of another Mighty Quinn! Brendan Quinn was much stronger, more determined than his brothers and he wouldn't allow himself to give in to such temptation. Once Amy was off his boat and out of his life, he'd be safe again. He just had to make sure that happened as quickly as possible.

AMY STRETCHED sinuously beneath the down comforter, enjoying the warmth that enveloped her body. She opened her eyes and glanced around the cabin, taking in her surroundings. Light poured through the small portholes, dust motes dancing in the drafts that swirled through the chill morning air.

She knew she was alone, yet hadn't recalled just when Brendan had crawled out of his bed. The clock on the bedside table read 9:00 a.m., a bit earlier than she usually rose after a night of waitressing at the Longliner. Amy sighed. But she was no longer a waitress. Today, she'd have to go out and find another job and another place to live, someplace clean and affordable. She'd have to play the games that she'd learned to play so well, hiding her real identity, employing clever strategies that would thwart the private detectives hired to find her.

Though the thought of starting all over again was a hassle, it was part of the life she'd chosen, a life filled with new experiences and adventures. In the six months since she'd left home, Amy had never once regretted her decision to run away. She paused. Well, maybe once or twice, when she thought about her grandmother.

Adele Aldrich was—and always would be—the single most important influence in Amy's life. Her father's mother had never resigned herself to the role her own parents had groomed her for. At age eighteen she'd received her trust fund and had immediately set off on a round of scandalous adventures—a safari in Africa, a trek through the Andes, even a boat trip down the Amazon. Then, to her parents' dismay, she learned how to fly and lent those skills to the war effort in England.

Amy smiled. "I'm having my adventure, Grandmother," she murmured. "But it would be a whole lot easier with money in my pocket."

She sat up and grabbed the down comforter, wrapped it around her shoulders, and went in search of Brendan. Maybe she could convince him to give her just one more night here. It wasn't easy to find a job that met all her criteria—no government forms, cash instead of a paycheck and meals included. Finding a place to stay was even harder. With only thirty dollars to her name, she barely had a few days' rent, much less a deposit.

When she reached the main cabin, Brendan was nowhere to be found. Amy walked back and listened at the door of the head. Then she opened the door to her cabin and found him curled up in her berth, blankets twisted around his waist and his chest bare. For a moment, she forgot to breathe, startled once again by how handsome he was.

Luckily she'd been able to put thoughts like those out of her mind last night. Sharing a bed with a complete stranger was one thing. But sharing a bed with the sexiest man she'd ever met was quite another. Maybe it was best that she leave today. Her life was complicated enough already. Involving a man in it— even a man as desirable as Brendan Quinn—would only make things worse.

With a soft sigh, she gently laid the down comforter on top of him and wandered back to the main cabin. She had felt safe here, at least for one night. Amy tossed off her gloves and set out to make a pot of coffee. Before long, the rich smell filled the cabin and she poured herself a mug and sat down at the table.

Idly, she flipped through a stack of papers slowly realizing that she was looking at a book manuscript. Beneath another pile was a book jacket. She pulled it out and found herself staring at a picture of Brendan

Quinn, looking slightly dangerous, like a modern-day pirate. "Bestselling author of *Mountain Madness*," she murmured. A list of quotes by other authors gave glowing reviews of Brendan's last book about a rescue on the north face of Mount Everest.

She went back to the manuscript and slid it in front of her. This book wasn't about mountain climbing. It was about the men and women she'd come to know while working at the Longliner. The commercial fishermen who fished the North Atlantic and the families who waited for them to come back from the sea.

Amy was drawn immediately into the story, Brendan's prose illuminating the reasons why men fished, why they risked their lives every day in a dangerous job to make a living that was backbreaking and often heartbreaking. Characters came to life and she recognized many of the qualities that her customers at the tavern possessed. Though the fishermen were a hard-living bunch, Brendan gave them all a quiet dignity as he explained how their way of life was slowly disappearing.

On and on she read, pouring a fresh cup of coffee for herself when her first cup got cold. As she read, she not only got to know the fishermen of Gloucester, she also learned more about the author—about what he respected and what he cherished in life, about the way he looked at the world.

"What are you doing?"

Amy jumped at the sound of his voice, pressing her palm to her chest. "You scared me," she said.

His expression was cool with just a hint of aggravation. She put the manuscript down, realizing that she'd made a mistake in looking at it at all. "I'm sorry. I just picked it up and started reading. I didn't mean to do anything wrong. It's just that once I started, I couldn't stop." Amy smiled up at him. "It's a wonderful book."

He shifted, clearly surprised by her compliment. His eyes were still sleepy and his hair mussed, and the stubble of beard that had shadowed his face the night before looked even more rakish. He wore only a pair of jeans and Amy couldn't help it when her eyes returned again and again to his broad chest and muscled belly. How could he possibly be so perfect, she wondered. There had to be a flaw somewhere.

"I didn't mean to snoop," she said with a light laugh. "I'm just a curious person. I always have been."

He shrugged. "It's not finished yet."

"I know," Amy said, picking up the pages and flipping through them. "If you ask me, the book needs a bit more depth. I wanted to know more about the personal lives of these men, what they wanted to be when they grew up, what their dreams were. Why they decided that fishing was their only option in life. And their wives and their friends, I wanted to know them, too. Did you ever think about interviewing them? It might add more color to your story." She stopped short, realized that she might have insulted him. Why was she always so quick to give her opinion, even when it wasn't requested? "Not that it needs more color. It's very colorful as it is." She drew a deep breath. "I really don't know what I'm talking about, so just ignore me. Besides being a snoop, I often stick my foot in my mouth."

Brendan stared at her for a long moment. "You

know something about writing," he said. "You have good instincts."

She smiled at the compliment. "I studied American literature in college." The smile wavered. "Before I dropped out, that is. And I read a lot. Fashion magazines, mostly." It wouldn't do for him to think she was *too* smart. He might start to ask questions.

"Where did you go to college?" Brendan asked as he moved to pour himself a mug of coffee.

"A small junior college near Los Angeles," Amy lied. She made a mental note to keep her story straight. Her family was on the West Coast, though she hadn't named a definite location. Now, she claimed to attend a nameless junior college in California. "You know, I could help you with your book. I noticed that you have all these notes and they're very disorganized. I could type and proofread and make suggestions. I could be your assistant."

He laughed. "I don't need an assistant," Brendan said, raking his hands through his hair as he took a place across the table from her.

She picked up the notes he'd scribbled on Longliner cocktail napkins. "I think you do. From what I can tell, you still need to check facts and there are some gaps in your research. And once you finish this book, you must have other projects. I could help you with all of that. Besides you do owe me."

His eyebrow rose. "Owe you?"

"It's because of you that I lost my job. And my place to stay."

He stared at her for a long moment and hope began to grow in her heart. Was he actually considering her proposal? And if she did become his assistant, did that mean she could continue to stay on his boat? "All right," he finally said. "Just for grins, let's say I did need an assistant. What sort of compensation would you expect?"

"Three hundred dollars a week," Amy said firmly. "Cash. Plus a place to stay."

Brendan shook his head. "Three hundred dollars a week? I'm not a rich man. Besides, if I paid you that much, then I'd sure as hell want to deduct it on my taxes. One hundred dollars a week in cash."

"Two-fifty," Amy countered, then quickly amended it to two hundred. "Cash and a place stay. And that's my final offer."

"Two hundred cash and a place to stay?"

"Yes," she said. "That's what I was making at the bar."

Brendan drew a deep breath and let it out slowly. Amy waited, silently praying that she hadn't made a mistake by asking for too much. "All right," he said. "But for two hundred—cash—you do anything I ask."

She frowned, her eyes narrowing. "Oh, no," Amy said, pushing to her feet. "I may be desperate, but I'm not that—"

"That's not what I mean," Brendan said.

"What *do* you mean?"

"I'm not talking about sexual favors," he replied. "If you're going to be my assistant, then I may ask you to take care of some things that might not be writing-related. Like grocery shopping or running errands or cleaning up the galley. An assistant needs to be prepared to do anything to make a writer's life easier."

"I can do that," Amy said.

"And you sleep in your own cabin. I'll get you some new blankets and a space heater. And you ask before you snoop through my things. I value my privacy. I'm not used to having people around and I don't want you to get underfoot."

"All right," Amy said. Though she made the promises, she didn't intend to keep all of them. She'd always been a naturally curious person, so snooping was part of her nature. She was also gregarious, so getting underfoot was just her way of socializing. And after one night in Brendan Quinn's bed, Amy had the distinct impression that it wouldn't be her last. "But I have one request. I mean besides two hundred a week and a place to stay and a new down comforter of my own."

"What is that?" Brendan asked.

She stared down at her coffee mug, trying to decide exactly what to tell him. Or whether to tell him at all. "If anyone comes around here, looking for me, no matter who it is, I want you to say that you don't know me and that you've never seen me before in your life. Can you do that?"

"Someone's going to come here looking for you?" he asked. "Who?"

"Never mind," she said. "Can you do that for me?"

"What's this all about?" Brendan asked, a suspicious edge to his voice. "Are you in trouble with the law?"

"No. I can honestly say, swear to God, that I'm not in trouble with the law. It's just a private matter that will work itself out over time."

"All right," Brendan said. "It's a deal."

With a tiny scream of joy, Amy jumped up and

grabbed him across the table, wrapping her arms around his neck and giving him a fierce hug. "I would have done it for nothing," she cried. "Anything so I wouldn't have to take another waitressing job." She stepped back. "But I'll do a good job. I swear. You won't have any complaints."

"I hope not," Brendan murmured. He picked up his coffee and stood as if he needed to put some space between them.

Amy gave him an apologetic smile. "Right. You're a very private person and I probably shouldn't have done that."

Brendan turned and grabbed a leather case from a locker in the main cabin and set it on the table. "You can use this laptop," he said. "You do know how to use a computer, don't you?"

"Of course," she replied, unzipping the case.

He grabbed two microcassettes and a recorder from the counter in the galley and set them down beside the case. "These need to be transcribed. Typed, double-spaced. After you're done with that, you can arrange these interview notes by subject. Then you can take this list and run to the grocery store. We're going to be working late and we'll need a lot of coffee. And you'll need to buy whatever you like to eat for breakfast, lunch and dinner. Can you cook?"

"No. But I have a very good instinct for takeout. I can tell by just reading the menu whether the food will be great or mediocre. You're paying for my meals, right?"

Brendan chuckled. "You drive a hard bargain, Ms. Aldrich."

She sent him a sly grin. "I suppose I do, Mr. Quinn."

"I've got to run into Boston," Brendan said. "I'll be back sometime later this afternoon." He reached in his wallet and pulled out fifty dollars. "For the groceries." With that, he took his coffee and walked back to his cabin. When she heard the door snap shut behind him, Amy did a little jig around the room, giggling with excitement.

This was perfect. It was everything she could have hoped for. She had a job and a nice place to stay. Her employer was just about the most handsome man she'd ever met. And though he refused to admit it, there was a tiny spark of attraction between them. Who knows where that might lead, she mused. Wherever it eventually did lead, it sure would be an adventure getting there!

BRENDAN HEFTED the box of books onto his shoulder, balancing it carefully before he started up the front steps of Dylan's flat. "This will be something new," he called to Conor. "Books in Dylan's apartment. I guess he'll have to throw away his collection of girlie magazines to make room."

Meggie Flanagan, Dylan's fiancée, stood on the porch, her hands braced on her hips, her cheeks rosy from the cold. "We already got rid of them," she teased, slapping Brendan's arm playfully as he passed. "Now if I could only get rid of that awful leather recliner, I'd be happy."

Dylan emerged from the front door and grabbed her from behind, giving her a playful kiss on the neck. "I haven't really showed you what we can do in that recliner," he teased. "You may come to appreciate it much more."

Moving day had been planned for almost two weeks and it was a tradition in the Quinn family that hiring professional movers was a waste of money—especially when a guy had five strong and willing brothers to do the job. It had never been a chore, since the six brothers enjoyed each other's company—and they didn't change their addresses that often. Besides Brendan hadn't seen any of his brothers since Conor and Olivia's wedding and it was nice to catch up.

Brendan grinned at Meggie. "Yeah, wait till he shows you how he can balance a beer can on one arm and a bowl of chips on the other while he wields the remote. You'll never love him more."

Meggie's giggle followed him as he slowly climbed the stairs to the second-floor flat. Though Brendan hated to admit it, the more time he spent with Dylan and Meggie—and Conor and Olivia—the more he was beginning to feel like an outsider in his own family. Just a few months ago, all six Quinn brothers were happily unattached—and planning to stay that way. Now, it was as if some disease had befallen the two oldest sons. Conor had already made a trip to the altar and Dylan was due to march to his doom sometime in June. But they didn't act like men who had succumbed to some disaster. Instead, they behaved as if they shared a special secret that they weren't telling anyone else.

Brendan certainly didn't begrudge his brothers their happiness. But he had to wonder how they could have turned from confirmed bachelors into lovestruck fools in such a short time. Brendan couldn't imagine the same thing happening to him. He'd always been able to keep the women in his life in proper perspective— separate from his career and the life he had chosen to lead. He had thought his brothers possessed the same talent, but he'd obviously been wrong.

"You haven't said much today," Conor commented, stepping up behind him to help him lower the box of books to the floor. "Everything going all right with the book?"

"Fine," Brendan said, wiping his hands on the thighs of his jeans.

"No problems getting it all done?"

"Not anymore. I've hired an assistant to help me out."

Conor blinked in surprise. "You've never had an assistant before," he said. "Why now?"

Brendan smiled. He really hadn't intended to tell anyone about Amy. But there were certain concerns he had, concerns that Conor, a police detective, might help to alleviate. "She just stumbled across my path and she needed a job, so I gave her one."

Conor stared at him for a long moment, then walked into the kitchen and retrieved a couple of bottles of beer from the refrigerator. Using the front of his T-shirt, he twisted one open and handed it to Brendan, then opened the other for himself. "You just gave her a job?"

Brendan nodded, taking a quick sip of the cold beer. Even though the temperature outside was below freezing, climbing up and down the stairs with heavy boxes had worked up a decent sweat. "Yeah, I know it sounds a little rash. But I was partly responsible for getting her fired from her regular job. And getting her kicked out of the room she was renting. I felt a responsibility to give her a place to stay for the night." He shrugged. "Then, all of a sudden, she talked me into offering her a job. I pay her in cash, give her a place to stay and she's at my beck and call."

Conor leaned against the doorjamb to the kitchen and studied Brendan shrewdly. "What kind of job did she have before?"

"She was slinging drinks at a waterfront dive in Gloucester," Brendan said.

"She was a cocktail waitress?"

"No, that would have been a step up from what she was doing."

Conor's frown deepened. "She's not a stripper, is she? Because I worked vice and let me tell you, strippers are—"

"No!" Brendan interrupted. "She's not a stripper. Just some girl trying to make a living. But that's the weird thing. She didn't belong in that bar with that crowd. She's...different."

"How so?"

"She's well read, she's bright, she's clever and she talks like she grew up on Beacon Hill, very cultured. But she has this...wild side."

Conor stared down at his beer and picked at the label with his fingernail. "I hate to state the obvious here, but this girl sounds like a first-rate con artist. You offer her a place to stay for a night and she moves into your life."

"That's kind of the way I saw it, too. That's why I was hoping you could check her out."

"Check her out?" Conor asked.

"Yeah, do that police detective stuff that you do. You used to work in vice, you've still got friends there. Find out who she is and where she came from. Her name is Amy Aldrich. She's blond, though I'm pretty sure it's not natural, with blue eyes. And she's got a really nice figure. Slender but curves in the right places. About five foot five and maybe one hundred and fifteen tops. And she wears lots of earrings."

"Lots of earrings?" Conor asked. "That's it? That's all you can give me? Lots of earrings?"

"That's all I have," Brendan replied. "What more do you want?"

"Well, if you really want to know, go through her stuff. Send her on an errand that doesn't require her purse and go through her wallet. Look for clues in her luggage. Try to find a driver's license or a credit card, anything I can trace."

"Her luggage," Brendan said. "There was a clue there, though I didn't think much of it at first. She had monogrammed luggage, the really expensive leather kind. And the monogram was *A-A*. For Amy Aldrich. But then there was an *S* on the end."

"Maybe she's married."

Conor's words were like a punch to the stomach. Could she have a husband somewhere? Was that who she was running from? Brendan swallowed hard. "She sure doesn't act married."

"And what's that supposed to mean?" Conor asked. "How does a woman act married?"

"You know. Like Olivia. All happy and content with herself. Focussed. That's the thing about Amy. She just doesn't seem to have a plan. And she made me promise that if anyone came around looking for her, to tell them that I don't know her."

"She's married," Conor said. "She's married and for some reason she's on the run. If you know what's good for you, Bren, you'll fire her. Get her off your boat and out of your life for good. Before her ex-con husband shows up with a gun."

"Yeah, but if she's got a violent husband, then isn't she safer with me?"

Conor stared at him for a long moment. "Aw, hell. Don't tell me you're falling for this girl."

"No way!" Brendan said. "Absolutely not!"

"You are," Conor insisted. "You know, I thought when you finally found someone, I'd be happy for you. But this girl is not *the* girl, Bren. Trust me on this. The minute you started describing her, my cop instincts went on alert. Cut her loose and find someone else to do your typing."

"Cut who loose?"

Brendan and Conor turned to find Dylan standing in the middle of the dining room, another box in his arms. He set it down on the dining room table then sighed. "When we decided to live here, I didn't realize Meggie had so much stuff," Dylan muttered. "We should have given up both places and found a bigger apartment."

"Why didn't you?"

"Because her parents don't know we're living together." Dylan raked his hand through his hair. "I feel like a teenager, sneaking around behind their backs. But Meggie wants a big wedding and so does her mother. We've been talking about getting married at the courthouse at Christmas, then having the wedding this summer, so we'll be legal." He reached down and opened the box, then began to pull out dishes wrapped in newspaper. "So who are you cutting loose?"

Brendan groaned inwardly. This conversation wasn't meant to become a family forum. Once Dylan and Conor knew, then Meggie and Olivia would know, and they'd tell Sean, Brian and Liam. Then it would be all around Quinn's Pub that Brendan Quinn had been duped by a pretty woman. "No one," Brendan said, sending Conor a warning look. "Just some girl I met."

"Not serious, huh?" Dylan asked.

"Not even close," Brendan replied.

"Good," Dylan said. "Because Meggie has a friend she'd like you to meet. Her business partner, Lana. She's blond, she's gorgeous, she's got a killer body."

Brendan held out his hand to stop his brother. "No, I'm not interested in having a woman in my life right now. I've got this book to finish and then I have a job in Turkey for four months writing a book about an archaeological dig. Maybe when I get back."

"You'll meet her at the wedding. She's going to be Meggie's maid of honor." Dylan wadded up some of the crumpled newspaper, then tossed it in a corner near the window. "I'd better get back downstairs and watch for Liam and the twins. They should be here with the last load by now." He looked at Brendan. "You're going to stay for pizza, aren't you?"

Brendan shook his head. "Naw, I better get back to Gloucester. I've got a lot of work to do."

Conor's brow quirked up and Brendan knew what

he was thinking. As far as his brother was concerned, the first order of business would be to boot Amy Aldrich off his boat. The second order of business would be to convince himself that he'd done the right thing.

After that, he'd occupy his time trying to forget the most beautiful, enigmatic and captivating woman he'd ever met.

3

"AMY!"

The sound of her name shouted across the crisp af-ternoon air caused Amy to stop short. Not many peo-ple knew her by name in Gloucester and she preferred to keep it that way. When she turned to find Serena, a former co-worker at the Longliner, waving at her from across the street, Amy breathed a silent sigh of relief. She waved back and waited while Serena crossed.

"Hi," her friend said breathlessly.

"Hi," Amy replied. "What's happening?"

Serena didn't bother with pleasantries, a concerned look wrinkling her brow. "Ernie's been asking about you."

Ernie was the daytime bartender at the Longliner and a father figure of sorts. He liked to watch out for Amy. He'd been the one to get her the room upstairs from the bar and he'd been the one to sneak her free meals during the day. "Ernie? What does he want? If he wants me to come back, you can tell him it's okay. I've already got a new job and a place to stay."

"You mean you're giving it all up?" Serena teased, her bright red curls bouncing as she talked. "And here I thought you enjoyed getting pawed by horny fisher-men."

"The tips were good, but not that good."

"Well, Ernie didn't want to talk to you about your job," Serena said. "He wanted to tell you that some guys in suits came looking for you at the bar early this morning. I stopped in to get my paycheck and I saw them. They looked like cops. Or the IRS. They asked if I knew where you were."

"Did you tell them?"

Serena shook her head. "No. I didn't know where you were. That's what Ernie told them, too. He said you were fired last night and for all he knew, you'd already moved on. Ernie hates cops. And he hates the IRS even more. He has issues with authority figures. So why are they looking for you? Are you in some kind of trouble?"

"Just the usual," Amy lied. "A few bad checks and some back rent. I was married to a real creep. When I left, I cleaned out the savings and sold the car."

Serena laughed. "I did the same thing when I left my ex-scumbag. Listen, I'm not going to tell a soul where you are. And once I warn the rest of the girls, they won't either. If you like, we could say that you moved to Michigan."

"That would be good," Amy said. "Listen, I've got to get back to work. I don't want to get fired my first day on the job."

"Stop by the bar sometime, I'll buy you a drink."

"I will," Amy said. "And thanks. Thanks for keeping my secrets."

Serena nodded, then ran back across the street. Amy watched her for a long moment, a sliver of guilt niggling at her. She hated to lie, but she had to consider the consequences of telling the truth. Her father's detectives were very well paid and would stop at nothing to find her. If they took off for Michigan, hot on her trail, she'd be safe for at least a few more weeks.

She started toward the dock, the plastic grocery bags swinging at her sides. But as she walked, she noticed two men standing across the street. Dressed in suits and trench coats, they looked completely out of place on the Gloucester waterfront—like cops or IRS.

Amy tried to tell herself that she was just being paranoid. But Serena had mentioned the suits in the bar and... As if they could read her thoughts, the two men looked up, their gazes focusing on the spot where she stood. Amy paused for a moment, wondering whether to just walk away casually or to run as fast as her legs would carry her. She chose the latter.

There was only one place to run. Down the maze of docks, between the smattering of boats still there. But as she ran, Amy knew she was trapped. She'd either have to find a boat on which to hide or give up. She paused and listened to the thunder of footsteps on the wooden piers. They were getting closer.

She looked both ways, then hurried toward a rusty old scow tethered to the west side of the dock. But there was no way to get up onto the boat. She cursed softly. There was only one choice if she wanted to avoid the men. She looked down into the water, knowing that it was probably cold enough to knock her unconscious. But it was her only chance at escape.

Grabbing a deep breath, she stepped off the edge of the pier and dropped into the water, groceries and all. The shock was enough to steal every bit of breath from her chest. She wheezed and gasped trying to take in air. The groceries were floating so she decided not to let go. She kicked over to a ladder at the end of the pier and moved around the backside of it so she couldn't be seen.

Then she waited while the footsteps passed up above her head, retreated and then came again. Her teeth chattered uncontrollably. If she thought she had been cold last night, she didn't know what cold was. This was excruciating! For a moment, she was sure she'd pass out. She began to count—thirty seconds, sixty seconds, ninety seconds—listening for sounds of the men in suits.

Amy waited for a full three minutes. Then, with the grocery bags looped over her arms, she struggled to crawl up the ladder. When she finally got to the top, she just wanted to lay on the dock for a few minutes and rest. But she knew the men could still be looking for her.

She stumbled down the dock toward *The Mighty Quinn*. When she reached the boat, she just didn't have the energy to haul herself onboard. With a soft cry, she sat down on the crate and waited for the men to return. "I can't do this," she murmured, trembling with the cold. This was it. They were going to find her and take her back to her family and she'd have to explain why she'd run away in the first place. There would be arguments and accusations and recriminations and the guilt would be heaped on so thick that she'd be forced to play the dutiful and grateful daughter again. Her new life was over.

"Amy?"

She jumped up, ready to run again, but the grocery

bags pulled her right back down. Firm hands grabbed at her shoulders and drew her to her feet. She was too weak and too cold to fight. She looked up, ready to admit defeat, but then she focused on familiar gold-green eyes. "Br—Brendan?"

"Amy, what the hell happened to you?" he said, untwisting the grocery bags from her wrists and letting them drop to the dock.

"I—I fell in," she said through her chattering teeth. "I'm-m-m all w-w-wet."

He picked her up and lifted her onto the deck of *The Mighty Quinn* then jumped on after her. "Come on, we need to get you inside and out of those clothes."

Amy struggled down the steps to the main cabin, then stood just inside the door, her body trembling with the cold, her limbs suddenly paralyzed. Her hair lay in strings around her face and little puddles formed around her feet. Brendan pulled her along to his cabin and before she could protest, he began to strip off her sodden clothes.

"You're soaked to the skin," he murmured, "and you're half-frozen."

"I—I fell in," she repeated, her teeth still chattering. "I—I did. I fell in." As he began to unbutton her shirt, Amy tried to brush his hands away, but her fingers were too stiff to do the job herself. She just wanted to get warm and the only way to do that was to allow Brendan to undress her. Besides, he clearly had undressed a woman before. He was quite adept at it.

"Close your eyes," she demanded as he set to work on the buttons again.

"What?"

"You can't just undress me," Amy said.

"The hell I can't," Brendan replied, skimming the wet blouse off her shoulders and arms. "Besides, you don't have anything I haven't seen before." To prove his point, he let his gaze drift slowly along her body, pausing briefly at the damp scraps of satin and lace that was her bra.

Amy's icy lips curled into a tiny smile as she crossed her arms over her chest. "Don't be so sure."

"Well, then, maybe I should look." He sent her a wicked grin before moving on to the rest of her clothes. He knelt down and yanked off her shoes and socks, then unbuttoned her jeans. Wrapping his fingers around the waistband, he peeled the clinging denim from her body. She stood in front of him, nearly naked, shivering, wearing nothing but goose bumps and underwear made transparent by the water.

"You don't have to stare," Amy murmured.

He chuckled softly and glanced up at her. "It's difficult not to, Ms. Aldrich. You look so..."

Amy waited for the words—incredibly sexy, devastatingly beautiful, undeniably desirable. He straightened, staring at her for a long moment. His thumb brushed along her lower lip in a tantalizing caress and for a moment, she thought he might kiss her.

"Blue," he finally murmured.

Amy gasped. "Blue?"

"Yes. You look blue." He grabbed a thick terrycloth towel from a locker behind him and wrapped her body in it, then pulled her against him, rubbing her back and her arms. "I suppose you're going to blame this on me, too."

Amy buried her face in the soft flannel of his shirt, inhaling the scent of soap and aftershave. "Well, if you didn't live on a boat, then I wouldn't have been in the vicinity of water. So I guess this could be your fault. Yes, in fact, I think I will blame this entirely on you."

He stepped back and gazed down into her eyes, then gently brushed a damp strand of hair off her forehead. "Here," he said, handing her another towel. "Wrap up your hair and crawl under the covers. I'll go make you some soup."

When he'd closed the door behind him, Amy did as she was told, tossing aside the towel wrapped around her body, then stripping out of her damp underwear. She rummaged through a chest at the end of the bed until she found one of Brendan's T-shirts. She slipped it over her naked body, then jumped into his bed and pulled the covers up around her nose.

Amy pinched her eyes shut, willing her body to warm up. She couldn't seem to stop shaking, no matter how tightly she pulled the comforter around her body. But was it all from the cold or was there a bit of fear mixed in? This was the closest she'd ever come to getting caught and Amy had to admit, she had been ready to give up—until Brendan had rescued her.

Funny how he always seemed to be there when she needed him the most. He'd been there in the bar and on the dock. And then here, in the cabin, to help peel the wet clothes from her shivering body. If she hadn't been so cold, she might just have been able to enjoy the moment. Maybe she might have given him a kiss—in gratitude, of course.

Amy shivered again at the thought. He had incredibly expressive hands and if she hadn't been completely numb, she was certain that his touch would have been undeniably erotic. For a moment, she'd imagined him undressing her for completely different reasons and those images alone made her blood run just a bit warmer. That was the best way to get warm, she mused. Think about seduction, Brendan slowly undressing her, running his hands over her body, tracing a path across her warm skin with his lips and tongue, lying on top of her body and...

She swallowed hard. Somehow, she knew that sex with Brendan Quinn would be wonderfully intense, filled with overwhelming sensation and heart-stopping desire. Just once in her life, she'd like to experience that feeling of raw, unadulterated passion. She'd never been lucky enough to feel that sensation. First, there had been the college boyfriends, fumbling and bumbling through the process. And then there had been her fiancé, a man whose idea of adventure was to do it on the bedroom floor.

Amelia Aldrich Sloane had been born for adventure. Running away from her rich and privileged life had been a start. Bleaching her hair blond and getting her ears triple-pierced had made a statement. Taking a job at a rowdy waterfront bar had been a bold move.

But having a passionate and thrilling little affair with Brendan Quinn—that would be the best adventure of all.

BRENDAN GRABBED the groceries from where he'd left them on the dock, drained the seawater out of the bags, then carried them down into the main cabin.

Though he tried to keep his mind on making soup, he couldn't help but return to what had happened just a few minutes earlier in his cabin.

He'd come home from Dylan's place fully prepared to give Amy her walking papers. He'd even decided to offer her severance pay, a few hundred dollars to tide her over until she found a new job and a permanent place to live. But the moment he saw her sitting on the crate next to his boat, his only thought was to get her warm and safe.

He didn't for one second believe that she'd fallen in the water by accident. Either she'd jumped or someone had pushed her. Brendan knew the answers would probably not come from Amy, so he was left to guess what had happened. If she'd been pushed, then she was definitely in danger. With the water as cold as it was, a person could die from hypothermia in a matter of minutes. If she'd jumped, she must have been awfully scared of something or someone. The shock of hitting the water wasn't something any human would voluntarily experience.

Though Brendan knew a rational man might distance himself from trouble, he felt compelled to protect her, even if it was from a crazy, gun-toting husband. She seemed so determined at times, almost as if she was desperately trying to lose herself in a world she was ill-equipped to handle. After being raised on tales of the Mighty Quinns, his first instinct was to come to her aid.

Brendan grabbed a can of soup from one of the grocery bags and opened the lid. He dumped it into a pan, added water, then slowly stirred. He'd let her stay for now—at least until Conor came back with solid information about her. Only then would he make a decision. And until that time he would have to ignore any attraction or desire he felt for her.

The chicken noodle soup heated quickly and he poured it into a large mug, grabbed some crackers and a spoon and headed back to his cabin. When he opened the door, he expected her to be sitting up, waiting for him. But she was curled beneath the covers, the down comforter pulled up over her head.

Brendan sat down at the edge of the bed. "Amy?" he said tugging on the comforter. When he pulled it back, he found her wrapped in an old T-shirt of his, curled up in a tight little ball and trembling with cold.

"I—I can't get warm," she murmured.

Brendan cursed beneath his breath. He knew enough about hypothermia to know that it was dangerous. "I should take you to the hospital," he said. "This could be serious. How long were you in the water?"

"Not that long," Amy replied. "Just get me another blanket."

But Brendan knew another blanket wouldn't help. There was only one thing left to do. He stood up and stripped off his jeans and his shirt, then climbed in beside her, pulling her naked backside into the curve of his lap and wrapping his arms around her. The cold of her body sucked the breath from his lungs and he winced, fighting the impulse to draw away.

"What are you doing?" she said, trying to wriggle out of his arms. "I—I don't have any clothes on underneath this shirt."

"Good," Brendan said. "I don't have any clothes on either. You'll warm up faster that way." He tried to keep his tone even and indifferent, as if holding a nearly naked woman in his arms was an everyday occurrence for him. He slowly rubbed her upper arms. Her skin was still so cold. "How's that?" he asked. "Better?"

"Mmm-hmm."

"We'll just wait a bit and then you can try some soup." He paused, allowing his hand to drift upward, beneath the sleeve of his T-shirt to her shoulder. He rubbed softly, enjoying the feel of her skin beneath his palms. Brendan fought the urge to press his lips against her nape. He closed his eyes and marshaled his hormones. He was wandering into dangerous territory. Maybe conversation would help. "Would you like to tell me what really happened?"

"I told you. I fell in the water," Amy said stubbornly. "Then I crawled out of the water. That's all."

"You don't have to keep secrets from me, Amy," he murmured, nuzzling his face into her damp hair. It smelled of salt water and the last traces of her shampoo. "You can trust me."

"I don't even know you," she countered.

"Well, we're lying here, with nothing to do but get warm. Why don't we get to know each other? Tell me something about yourself."

"Isn't this against the law?" she said impatiently. "A boss crawling into bed with an employee is considered sexual harassment, isn't it? I could sue you."

"A boss letting a valuable employee freeze to death

might be considered negligence. Now don't change the subject. We were talking about you."

She twisted in his arms and looked him in the eye. "Would you like to kiss me?" she asked.

Brendan stared at her uneasily, not sure that he'd heard her right. "What? Why would you ask that?"

Amy shrugged. "I was just curious. I mean, I'm almost naked and you're almost naked and we're lying in bed together. It's the next logical step, isn't it?"

Just the thought of kissing her, of pulling her body against his, her breasts pressed to his chest, her hips cradled in his, brought a flood of desire. There wouldn't be much foreplay involved in getting clothes off. Just a pull here and a tug there and nothing would stand between them but skin.

So much for self-control, Brendan thought. "I—I really don't think that would be a good idea," he murmured as he untangled his arms from around her body. He quickly crawled out of bed, grabbed his jeans and tugged them on, not bothering with the zipper. "Eat your soup," he said before he walked out the door.

When he got back to the main cabin, Brendan glanced around, not sure what to do with himself. He couldn't deny that he wanted to go right back in to Amy Aldrich and take her up on her offer. But could he stop at just one kiss? A kiss might lead to a caress and that would surely lead to other things more intimate, more erotic. Though the woman was exasperating and aggravating, she was also irresistibly sexy.

He cursed softly. She could also be married and Brendan drew the line at getting involved with a married woman. Hell, her marital status should be the least of his worries. She could be a felon, maybe even a convicted felon. He sat down at the table in the galley and raked his hands through his hair. Why couldn't he resist her? And how could they go from benign conversation about her background to—

Brendan cursed again as realization slowly dawned. She asked about the kiss on purpose! To divert his attention away from her accident and her past.

He strode back into the cabin and stood over his berth. Amy stared up at him, wide-eyed, the comforter pulled up to her nose. In one smooth movement, he leaned over her, his knee sinking into the mattress at her hip, his hands braced on either side of her head. "You asked if I wanted to kiss you?"

Amy's eyes went wide and she gave him a tiny nod.

He moved a bit closer. "I think you deserve an answer, don't you?"

She nodded again, lowering the comforter.

Brendan brought his mouth down on hers and kissed her. This wasn't just a casual kiss, a tentative brush of his lips. He kissed her with purpose, with the desire to make her heart beat faster. His tongue plundered her mouth, tasting deeply and exploring thoroughly. He stretched his body over the length of hers, trapping her. But she made no move to get away, gave no indication that she wanted it to end. He assumed she'd be shocked by his action but instead, she wrapped her arms around his neck and returned the kiss with equal intensity.

He knew he was lost the moment she responded. He'd kissed a lot of women in his life, but he'd never kissed a woman who seemed to enjoy it as much as Amy did. She was the kind of girl he could kiss for an hour or two, or maybe three, and not get bored, a girl whose mystery made her more tempting, more seductive.

It took a while for the impact of his miscalculation to set in. When he finally drew back, Brendan was certain that he shouldn't have kissed her—and just as certain that it would happen again. Having tasted her once he would want to do it again and again. He opened his eyes to find her smiling up at him. His gaze dropped to her lips, damp and slightly swollen, then fought the temptation to take more.

"I'm feeling much warmer now," she said. "Thanks."

He pushed off the bed, then turned to the door before his physical reaction to the kiss was more evident than his surprise at her reaction. "Good," he muttered. "Then I won't have to do that again."

When the door of his cabin closed behind him, Brendan stood in the companionway and reviewed the past few minutes of his life. He got the uneasy feeling that he was not the one in control here. But that was going to change. From now on, he'd think of Amy Aldrich as an employee and only as an employee—not as a beautiful, desirable, irresistible woman who kissed like a woman with passion on her mind.

THE DAWN was just breaking when Amy opened her eyes. At first she wasn't sure where she was. She'd been dreaming—a long, lazy, detailed dream about her bedroom back home, her huge four-poster bed, the thick pillows and soft blankets. There had been a time when she had felt content and happy there. But those feelings had changed when her parents had taken the side of a man she knew she couldn't trust.

The memory still brought an ache of betrayal to her heart. Shortly after their engagement she'd overheard her fiancé on the phone in an intimate conversation with a woman who was obviously more than a friend. Amy had confronted him and he'd denied everything, coming up with a plausible explanation for every question she posed. Her parents had leapt to his defense, claiming that Amy must have misunderstood. For a while, she'd convinced herself that she had.

But the mistrust wouldn't fade and as the wedding approached, every time she looked at Craig, she saw her life stretching out in front of her, filled with doubts and insecurities and regrets. Gradually, she came to realize that she'd never really lived her life for herself, never lived up to the potential that her grandmother saw in her.

When she walked out of her parents' home in the middle of the night, she'd been terrified, unsure that she was doing the right thing, concerned about how she'd survive on her own. Yet at the same time she'd been excited about the prospect of adventure and new experiences. Amy sighed softly. The adventure came at a price. It had been a long time since she'd felt truly safe. Now, for the first time since she'd left, she'd found a place where her doubts and fears faded. She was safe here on *The Mighty Quinn*...safe with Brendan Quinn. And she wanted to stay for just a little while.

She opened the door of her cabin and peeked inside.

He slept in the tiny berth, wearing a pair of sweat pants that rode low on his hips revealing a flat, muscular belly. One leg hung off the berth and he was covered only by a twisted section of a wool blanket, impervious to the damp chill that greeted the morning.

As she stared into his face, so boyish in sleep, a wave of gratitude washed over her. Brendan Quinn wasn't much more than a stranger, yet he'd taken her in, given her a place to stay and a way to make a living. A man would have to have a kind heart to do something like that. Amy drew in a slow breath. But then Craig had had a kind heart at one time—before her family's money corrupted him.

Amy brushed aside thoughts of her ex-fiancé and focused on Brendan, on the striking features of his face, the strong jaw, the chiseled mouth, the long dark lashes and the perfect nose. Her gaze fixed on his lips and she leaned closer, so close she was nearly touching him, wondering what it would be like to kiss him again.

Amy Aldrich had never been satisfied with "what ifs." She had become the queen of instant gratification. She leaned closer and brushed her mouth over his, allowing her tongue to trace the crease in his lips. A giggle slipped from her throat as a shiver raced through her. She knew it wasn't from the cold. It was the delicious sensation that came from doing something naughty.

The second time she kissed him, he opened his eyes and stared at her. At first, Amy thought he was still half-asleep and would close his eyes again. But then he reached up and wove his fingers through the hair at her nape and pulled her mouth against his in a long, deep, passionate kiss.

A tiny cry of surprise slipped from her throat, more from the startling intensity of the kiss than from the fact that he was wide awake. She recalled his promise of the night before and knew she was treading in dangerous territory. If Brendan Quinn had any thoughts at all about seducing her, she wasn't sure she'd be able to mount a decent defense—or if she even wanted to.

He grabbed her around the waist and rolled her over, his mouth still fixed to hers. His hand slipped up beneath the T-shirt then just barely brushed the curve of her breast, sending a wave of desire racing through her. She arched against him, offering him more, but his hand slid back down to her waist. Amy opened her eyes to find him staring at her.

"What are you doing?" he murmured, his breath warm against her lips, his tongue tasting and teasing.

She didn't really have an answer. Testing him was the closest she could come. Looking for a reaction. Wondering how far he was willing to go. "I'm kissing you," she said.

"Why?"

"Because it feels good?"

His gaze flitted over her face as if he were memorizing every detail. "I don't want you kissing me. And I don't want you sleeping with me. You're supposed to be my assistant. Nothing more."

Amy sighed and put on a playful pout. At the same time she ran her hand over his naked chest, reveling in the feel of hard muscle and smooth skin. "Then you don't like the way I kiss?"

He paused before he answered. "That's not what I said."

"Then you *do* like the way I kiss?"

"I have a feeling you've kissed a lot of men, Amy Aldrich and you don't take your kissing as seriously as I do. Or maybe you haven't kissed that many men and you don't realize the dangers involved in kissing."

"Actually, I haven't kissed very many men at all. That's why I'm so anxious to gain more experience whenever I can." Amy laughed softly. "Besides, how can you take kissing seriously? I mean, look at it. We both pucker up and press our lips together. Then we start in with the tongues. You can't take that seriously."

He leaned closer, his mouth hovering just a breath away from hers. "You obviously haven't been kissed by the right man," he murmured. "Because when it's done right, it's a very...very serious thing."

Amy held her breath, waiting, but he didn't move. "Show me," she challenged, her gaze fixed on his lips. What had begun as a playful experiment had turned exciting and dangerous. A wave of exhilaration washed over her and she longed to throw caution to the wind and take a chance.

"That would be a big mistake," he murmured, pushing away from her.

Amy groaned, then sat up and brushed her hair out of her eyes. "I don't know you well, Brendan Quinn, but I'd never have guessed you were such a prude." What kind of man would pass up an opportunity for intimacy, especially one so freely offered, Amy wondered. She crawled off the berth and stood up, determined to tweak his resolve. "If we're not going to have sex, then I suppose we should get to work," she said in a nonchalant tone. She grabbed the blankets and yanked them off the bed. "Get up. I need to get dressed and you have to get out of my cabin."

Brendan braced his elbows behind him and chuckled softly. "Who's the prude now? A few minutes ago you wanted to have sex and now you can't dress in front of me?"

"All right," Amy said, grabbing hold of the hem of her T-shirt with a wicked smile. "After all, it's not like you haven't seen it all before, right?"

In one quick movement, he jumped out of bed, twisted her hands around her back, and yanked her body against his. "You're playing a very dangerous game," he warned.

"Maybe I like danger," she replied.

He stared down at her, his expression tense, almost angry. "Who are you?" Brendan murmured. Reaching out, he cupped her face in his palm and pulled his thumb across her damp lips.

"I'm whoever you want me to be," Amy said.

"I want to know who you really are," he said. "I won't make love to an illusion."

As quickly as he grabbed her, he let her go, then turned and walked out of her cabin, closing the door firmly behind him. Amy hadn't realized that she was holding her breath until she gasped for air. Slowly, she sat down on the edge of the berth and pressed her palm to her chest. Her heart was pounding so hard she could hear it.

A tiny sigh slipped from her lips. When she'd run

away from her old life, she'd promised herself she was going to start living the way she wanted to live, experiencing every day as if it was an adventure. But making love to Brendan Quinn, though a tantalizing prospect, brought unwanted thoughts about what would come later.

She couldn't deny that she was attracted to him or that she was just a little curious about what it would be like to be swept away with passion. Though she knew consensual seduction would be an incredible experience, Amy wasn't sure she'd be satisfied with just one or two nights together. Brendan was the kind of man who'd be hard to forget. And she wasn't prepared to turn her future happiness over to yet another man.

There was also the money. What would happen when he found out about the money? Though most people believed that money could buy happiness, Amy knew better. That much money had never made her happy. People looked at her differently because she was Amelia Aldrich Sloane. They didn't see the person she was, only the money she'd inherit.

Well, Brendan Quinn was never going to look at her and see the heiress. He was never going to wonder just how much she was worth in monetary terms. She wasn't going to allow him to know that side of her. The Amy he'd pulled out of the Longliner that night was the real Amy. She'd stay with him for as long as she wanted and then she'd move on. But while she was here, she intended to live her life to the fullest and enjoy every pleasure that it offered—including the pleasure of kissing Brendan Quinn whenever she felt the urge.

4

BRENDAN SAT at the table in the galley of *The Mighty Quinn* and tried to focus his attention on the rewrites for his book. He'd been revising all morning, trying to make a chapter right that just didn't want to work. What it really needed was an interview with the widow of a swordboat captain lost at sea two years ago. But the woman had refused again and again to talk to him.

He turned his gaze up to Amy who had settled herself on one of the sofa berths in the main cabin. She hummed softly as she typed in edits he'd made on the previous chapter.

Over the past several days, since they'd shared their passionate early morning encounter, the tension between them had grown. It wasn't a bad tension born of anger or frustration. It was a tension drawn tighter by the question of when it would happen again, when they'd allow themselves another foolish lapse. Though Amy hadn't come to his bed since then, she hadn't exactly maintained a businesslike demeanor either.

Every now and then, as they worked together, she'd reach over and touch him—his hand, his arm, his shoulder. For a fleeting moment, he'd feel the same desire he'd felt when she was in his arms. Then it would be gone and he'd be left to wonder how such a simple

touch could cause such an intense and undeniable reaction—especially from a woman who remained an
enigma.

Who was she? And what was she running from?
Over and over again, he'd tried to figure out her story,
his mind running over wild scenarios. Yet in spite of
his doubts and reservations, he still found himself fan-
tasizing about her. At night, he'd lie awake, imagining
her body curled beneath her new down comforter, safe
behind her own cabin door...her hair rippling over the
pillow like spun gold, her skin warm and silken. It was
those times that he craved her body the most, the sup-
ple shape of her curves fitted against his. It was those
times when he had to fight the temptation to leave his
own berth and crawl into hers.

"This is good," she murmured, startling him out of
his thoughts.

"What?" Brendan asked, his gaze skipping from an
idle contemplation of her bare ankles to her face.

She held up a sheaf of papers. "This chapter is
good."

"But?" He always knew there was a "but." When it
came to his writing, she was an unforgiving judge. In
truth, Amy would make a hell of a book editor if she
ever gave up her career in waitressing. Her knowledge
of structure was beyond reproach. Her spelling was
impeccable as was her grammar. She had an uncanny
knack for the clean, tight narrative that he loved.

"No 'but,'" she said.

"You always have a 'but,'" Brendan countered.

"All right," she said. "*But* it would be better if you
could add the perspective of the captain's wife."

Brendan smiled tightly. Sometimes he wondered if she could read his mind. He knew that was precisely what was wrong with the book and it irritated him that she was able to see in just one reading what it had taken him months to discover. "I've tried to interview her but she refuses to talk to me."

"I could try," Amy suggested. "She might be more willing to talk to a woman. Besides, I know a lot of these women from the Longliner. Maybe I could get to her through a friend."

Brendan pushed up from the table, mildly irritated—but not at her honesty. Instead, it was because the whole time she was criticizing his writing, he was thinking about pulling her into his arms and kissing her senseless. Tracing a path from her mouth to her neck to her shoulder, until she moaned in surrender and went soft in his arms. "I'm going to take a walk. Clear my head."

Amy stood up. "I'll go with you," she said brightly. "I've been cooped up all day. It will be nice to get out and get some exercise."

Though Brendan really didn't want company, he had no way to dissuade her from coming. Once Amy Aldrich set her mind on something, there was no changing it. In such close quarters, he'd already learned it was better to bite his tongue than to argue with her.

She tugged on her boots, then grabbed her jacket and mittens before climbing out on deck. He followed her, jumped down to the dock first, then turned to grab her waist. She placed her hands on his shoulders as he swung her down. They stood for a long moment, her arms around his neck, his hands spanning her waist.

It would be so simple to bend closer and kiss her, to take just one taste and then retreat. But Brendan knew that one taste would never be enough. The last time he'd kissed her, he'd wanted so much more—and she'd been willing to oblige. He gave her an uneasy smile, then let his hands drop to his sides. "Let's go," he said. She nodded and looped her arm through his.

Gloucester was an unusual town, its working-class waterfront contrasted with Cape Anne's touristy atmosphere in the summer. But in the winter, everything was calmer and quieter, almost serene. The swordboats headed south into warmer waters, the sailors who kept their pleasure boats in the marinas hauled them out for winter maintenance and the tourists found climates more suitable to their tastes. Brendan liked the peace and often walked late at night when he was restless.

They strolled past taverns and shops and short-order restaurants, beneath lighted Christmas decorations hanging from every other lamppost. Amy tipped her face up and let the snow catch in her hair and her lashes. Brendan stared at her, convinced that she was the most beautiful woman he'd ever known.

"I love Christmas," Amy murmured. "It's my favorite time of the year."

For the first time since he'd met her, she'd revealed something personal about herself. "Why is that?" Brendan ventured.

"It's magic," she said. "I always remember the mornings I woke up and went downstairs and there was this huge Christmas tree that had arrived in the middle of the night, completely decorated, with lights and shiny glass ornaments and tinsel. And beneath it were presents all wrapped in the prettiest paper and topped with elaborate bows. My heart would start beating a little faster and it stayed that way until Christmas morning."

"You know" Brendan began, "that's the first time you've ever mentioned your childhood. I was beginning to think you didn't have one. That you just emerged from the womb fully grown."

Amy laughed softly, bumping playfully against his shoulder. "I had a childhood. And it was a very lovely one indeed."

"Then what changed?" he said.

"Changed?"

He thought carefully about his words, hoping to entice her into telling him more, anxious to know the truth about her. "You mentioned that you and your family don't speak. I got the impression that you were estranged. Why is that?"

"Nothing really," she said with a shrug. She stared up at the sky. "I think we're going to get a big snowstorm tonight." She drew a deep breath. "It smells like snow."

They walked another half block in silence, Brendan's frustration growing. But then something seemed to catch her attention in the window of the hardware store across the street. She grabbed his hand and pulled him along.

"Look," she cried, pointing to the boxes of Christmas lights and ornaments stacked in the windows. "Let's get some decorations for the boat."

He shook his head. "I'm really not much for Christmas."

"It will be fun! Kind of like Venetian night. I remember one Christmas my parents and I were in—" She stopped suddenly. "You know what I mean, when they decorate all the sailboats with lights and then they have a big parade on the water?"

Brendan stared at her for a long moment, catching the flicker of worry that passed through her expression almost as if she'd said something she shouldn't have and now she wished she could take it back. A Venetian night in the middle of winter. One didn't see sailboats draped with Christmas lights in South Boston or Gloucester in December. One saw them in Palm Beach or Santa Barbara—or Venice, Italy. "I don't know if I'm going to be around for Christmas," he said.

She looked over at him, her eyes wide. "Where are you going to be?"

Brendan shrugged. "I don't know. The book will be done. I'll probably spend some time in Boston with my family then maybe take a vacation. Where are you going to be?"

She turned away, staring back into the hardware store window, her palms pressed to the plate glass window. "I guess I assumed I'd still be working for you. Your book isn't due until January. And I thought, after that you'd..." Amy smiled. "Never mind. You should be with your family."

Brendan fought the urge to reach out and turn her gaze toward his. He'd assumed that she'd known the job was short-term, a few weeks at the most. She couldn't have expected to be his assistant permanently, could she? "Or maybe I'll be here," he said. "My family has never really done much for Christmas. Maybe that's why I'm such a Scrooge. And who knows if the book will be done by then."

"I thought everyone celebrated Christmas."

"Everyone does, except the Quinns. When I was a kid, my dad was never around at Christmas and we were too poor to believe in Santa Claus. Conor always made us go to midnight mass, which we loved. We each got one present to unwrap when we got home. But once we got older, we all kind of gave up on Christmas. There didn't seem to be much point."

"What about your mom?" Amy asked.

"She wasn't around either." He paused, an image of his mother flashing in his mind. "Fiona McClain Quinn. She left when I was four or five. I don't really remember much about her. I do remember once, we had a Christmas tree though. With big colored lights and an angel on the top. Or maybe I'm just imagining that memory."

"Well, you can make new memories," she said. "We could bake Christmas cookies and string popcorn. We could buy a few Christmas CDs. That would get you in the spirit pretty quick."

Brendan shook his head. "No, I don't think so. But, hey, if you want to go home for Christmas, you should do it. I can loan you some money. I can even help you out with a plane ticket. Maybe I could even get a discount on a flight for you."

Amy shook her head. "No, I can't. It's not the

money. I just...can't." She took a deep breath. "I'm sorry about your mom," she murmured.

"And I'm sorry I'm such a Scrooge," he said.

She gave him a sly smile. "I'm not convinced you are," she said. "I'm going to do my best to change your humbug ways. You'll see. By the twenty-fifth of this month, you'll know all the words to "Up On The Housetop" and you'll be able to spell *pfeffernüesse.*"

He laughed, glad that the mood had lightened. "*Pfeffernüesse?* I don't need to know how to spell a word that I can't even define."

"Don't tell me about your problems with spelling," she teased. "I'm the one who has to catch your mistakes."

He grabbed her around the shoulders and pulled her close, giving her a teasing hug. "That's what I have a spellchecker for on my computer. What you're finding is typing mistakes. My spelling is perfect."

"*Pfeffernüesse,*" Amy said, slipping out of his embrace and walking backwards in front of him.

"I wouldn't even know if *you* spelled it right, much less me."

"*P-F-E*-double-*F-E-R-N-U* with an umlaut-*E*-double-*S-E*," she said. "It's a German spice cookie with a powdered sugar coating. See, Mr. Scrooge, you can learn something besides 'bah, humbug.'"

Brendan stopped, then reached out and scooped up a handful of snow. He slowly packed it into a ball and tossed it in front of him. Her eyes went wide and her grin turned mischievous "Here's something else you can spell," he said. "How about 'direct hit.'"

"How about 'seriously deluded,'" she shot back.

With a tiny cry, she took off running down the sidewalk, slipping and sliding on the fresh coating of snow. He lobbed the snowball in her direction and it hit her on the back of the neck. She screamed, then hurried around the corner of a building.

Brendan approached slowly, knowing that she'd be lying in wait with a snowball of her own. He decided surprise was his best option. He counted to thirty, then drawing a deep breath, he stepped around the corner and roared at the top of his lungs.

The look on her face was sheer shock. She screamed again. Her hands flew up to her mouth and her snowballs hit *her* in the face, not him. Brendan grabbed her around the waist and laughed, watching the melting snow dribble down her cheeks. But his laugh faded as he stared down into her eyes.

With a soft moan, he brought his mouth down on hers. She opened beneath him, their tongues touching, hesitantly at first, and then desperately, as if they had craved the taste of each other for far too long. Brendan pushed her back against the brick wall of the building, bracing his hands on either side of her head.

"Your face is wet," he murmured, with a soft chuckle. "And cold."

Amy groaned and reached up to wipe off the melting snow. He grabbed her hand and gently pulled it away. Instead, he used his lips and his tongue to catch the water droplets trickling down her damp cheeks, a tantalizing way to explore her face. He forgot about his pledge to keep his distance, caught up in his desire and unable to deny himself just one taste.

As he caressed her face with his lips, she fumbled

with the front of his jacket, pushing her hands inside until she could smooth them across his chest. Then she worked at the buttons of his shirt, twisting them open one by one. When her palms pressed against warm skin, Brendan moaned. No woman had ever affected him the way Amy did. All she had to do was look at him, smile or murmur his name, maybe accidentally brush against him, and his mind would be paralyzed with need, consumed with thoughts of possessing her.

He lost track of where they were, ignoring the pedestrians that passed by, ignoring the cold wind that cut through their clothes. As far as he cared, they were completely alone and unable to stop themselves. Brendan leaned into her, his hips pressed against hers.

When she moved, sensation shot through him, desire pooling in his lap. "Why do you do this to me?" he whispered, his mouth dancing over hers.

"I like to torture you," she said. She grabbed his bottom lip between her teeth and bit just hard enough to prove to him who was really in control.

"You do like to torture me. In all sorts of ways."

She smiled coyly, then sucked on the spot that she'd just bitten. "But aren't you glad you hired me? I've worked very hard to make myself indispensable."

A shrill whistle split the air and then a shout. "Hey, buddy, get a room!"

Amy peered over Brendan's shoulder at a group of four brawny men. "We better go, before we get arrested."

"What we're doing isn't against the law," Brendan said, turning back to nuzzle her neck. Or maybe it was, he mused. Problem was, he didn't care anymore.

"Not now, maybe," she teased, dancing away from him with a laugh. "But I can't guarantee that what might happen later wouldn't be illegal in forty or fifty states. I think it's called public indecency. Or maybe lewd and lascivious behavior."

Brendan followed her down the street, dodging the snowballs she tossed his way. He thought back to the night he'd met her at the Longliner, the decision he made to pick her up and carry her out to the street. He had been sure that simple act would spell disaster for his life. And now that he'd been completely captivated by the unconventional beauty of Amy Aldrich, Brendan was beginning to believe he'd been right.

Though she still remained a virtual stranger, a woman without a past, he'd lost his ability to resist her charms. A little voice in his head told him to walk away, to trust his instincts. But the instincts that were warning him about Amy were balanced by those pushing him toward her.

He couldn't help but believe that the real disaster might have occurred if he'd never met Amy at all.

THE BOAT WAS SILENT, rocking gently at its moorings while the winter wind blew outside. Amy peered through the porthole at the gathering snow on the rear deck. Brendan had left early that morning for an interview with a Boston magazine. Although he'd left her plenty to do, she'd pushed her work aside in favor of pacing the length and breadth of the main cabin.

She'd grown so used to having Brendan around that she didn't feel safe without him close by. After last night's walk, they'd come back to the boat, but as soon as they'd stepped inside the main cabin, the impact of the intimacies they'd shared came into focus. A playful kiss on a snow-covered street was one thing, but unrestrained passion in the privacy of Brendan's boat was something entirely different. It would change things between them forever.

At first, Amy had thought that a night or two of passion was exactly what she needed, just another step in her quest for adventure and thrilling experiences. But that was when Brendan was nothing more than a handsome face and an incredibly sexy body. Now, he was a man who had the capacity to make her forget herself and the new life she was determined to build.

It wouldn't be hard to fall in love with a man like Brendan. He was solid, focused, a man who knew exactly who and what he was. He'd built his own life out of his talent for storytelling rather than relying on family money or connections. He was his own man, a man she found herself wanting more with every day they spent together.

Amy groaned, then peered out the porthole again. He'd promised to be back before lunch. They were going to make a research trip to the fish processing plant to learn more about the fluctuating prices of fresh North Atlantic swordfish. Amy had suggested that he add an economic slant to chapter seven and he'd found the idea intriguing.

"All right," Amy murmured. "Now, I'm bored. And when I'm bored, I do irresponsible things." She idly studied the titles of the books lining the shelves in the main cabin. Then she wandered into the head and opened the medicine chest, pulling out Brendan's razor, then his toothbrush, then his aftershave, examining each one as if they might offer a clue to the man she was living with.

Amy tossed the items back inside, then moved on to his cabin. She knew she shouldn't be snooping and that he had every right to his privacy. After all, she'd so closely guarded her own privacy and he'd respected that. But what harm was there in snooping? As long as she didn't get caught, he'd never know.

Glancing over her shoulder, she listened for a long moment for his footsteps on deck, then opened the drawer of his bedside table. With a smile, she picked up a harmonica, then blew softly on it, wondering if he could play. The drawer also held a box of condoms. She opened it up and noticed there were three missing. An unbidden surge of jealousy washed through her as she thought about the other women he'd shared his bed with. A search for the drugstore receipt proved fruitless. So she had no idea when he might have been with those other women.

A more detailed inventory of the drawer yielded nothing more except a bottle of aspirin, some ticket stubs to movies, a handheld game, an old driver's license and about a hundred pens and pencils. Amy sighed, then turned to the shelves that made up the headboard of his berth. This part really couldn't be considered snooping, since everything was right out in the open. And since she spent a few nights in his cabin, it was only natural that she might search for something to read.

She pulled out a spiral notebook and settled herself on the bed. Opening it, she recognized his handwriting immediately. At first she thought it was a diary and quickly shut it and put it back on the shelf. But curiosity was too strong to resist. Had he written anything about her?

She grabbed the notebook again, opened it on her lap and began to read. It wasn't a diary but a collection of stories, all about Irish heroes named Quinn. Her memory flashed back to their first night together. He'd mentioned stories of the Mighty Quinns, claiming that was the reason he'd rescued her at the Longliner. The book was filled with wonderful tales, all of them told with great imagination and vivid imagery. Amy found herself captivated, drawn into a world of knights and dragons and magical kingdoms.

"Hi."

Amy glanced up to find Brendan standing in the doorway of his cabin, snowflakes still dusting his hair and shoulders. She froze as she watched his gaze drop to what she was reading. With a soft curse, she shoved the notebook under the comforter.

His eyebrow arched. "What are you doing in my cabin?"

The heat rose in her cheeks and she sent him an apologetic smile. "I'm sorry. I was bored and I was looking for something to read and I found this notebook." She held it out to him. "These stories are wonderful."

"Where did you find that?"

"It was lying here among the magazines. I recognize some of the stories. They're from the Fenian Cycle, aren't they?"

"And the Ulster Cycle and the Mythological Cycle. And a few from the Cycle of Kings."

"But I don't remember all the heroes being named Quinn."

He smiled crookedly. "Well, that's a family tradition. We borrow liberally from Irish myths and take credit for heroic deeds that aren't ours." Brendan stepped into the cabin and took the notebook from her. He sat down on the edge of the berth and flipped through the notebook. "When I was kid, my da used to tell us these stories. He'd always substitute a Quinn ancestor for the hero. A Mighty Quinn he was called. The tales always focused on bravery and sacrifice, but whenever the Mighty Quinn fell in love, the story would end badly. Da thought this was a good way of teaching us not to trust women."

"Why would he do that?"

"Because my mother walked out on him. He never really recovered." Brendan pointed to the notebook. "I've been trying to remember the stories as we told them when I was a kid. I was thinking of putting them in a collection to give to my brothers."

"Do you ever hear from your mother?" Amy asked.

Brendan shrugged. "Da says she was killed in a car wreck about a year after she walked out. But Conor and Dylan never believed that story. I was really too young to know what was going on. All I knew was that one day she was there and the next day, she was gone."

"Do you remember what she looked like?"

"I know she had long dark hair, but I'm not sure if I know that because I remember it or because Conor and Dylan told me so. There were no photos in the house. But I do remember one thing. She used to wear a necklace with a kind of pendant. Conor described it to me once. It was a circle with hands clasped and a jewel in a little crown. When I'd sit with her, I'd always reach up and play with it."

"A *claddagh*," Amy said. "My grandmother has a *claddagh* ring. The two hands hold a heart and over the heart is a crown. It's an Irish symbol of love and friendship."

"That's it," he murmured, a faraway look coming into his eyes. "It was a *claddagh*."

Amy paused, a little sorry that she'd brought up such a painful subject. "You know, I could help you with the book," she offered.

Brendan leaned over and placed it back on the shelf on the headboard. "It's just something I was working on. Nothing to waste time over."

"Tell me one of the stories," Amy said.

He thought about her request for a long moment, then nodded. "All right." Brendan leaned back on the bed, bracing his elbows behind him. "But I have to put on a bit of Irish brogue to tell it right. It makes it sound better."

Amy flipped over on her stomach and lay beside him. "Go ahead."

"I'll tell you the story of Tadleigh Quinn, an imaginative boy who was always making up wild stories, telling anyone in his small village about the fairies and the gnomes and the sprites he'd see while wandering the woods. Of course, everyone knew Tadleigh to be a bit of a *sleeveen* and when they didn't believe his stories, he made them more elaborate and more fantastical. One day while Tadleigh was wandering in the woods, as he was wont to do most every day, he came across a beautiful princess imprisoned in a golden cage which hung from the highest branch of a tall oak tree."

"Oh, I love these kind of stories," Amy said. "Like *Sleeping Beauty* and *Rapunzel* and *Snow White*. I love it when the handsome prince comes to rescue the fair maiden."

"Tadleigh climbed up to the top of the tree and sat next to the cage, imagining what the villagers would say when he told them *this* story, how he had rescued a fair princess and in return, she'd given him a bag of gold—for she'd promised that he would be handsomely rewarded. Tadleigh tried desperately to free the princess, but the lock was heavy and the bars of the cage made of iron. 'I must go for help,' he said. But the princess cried out to stop him. She explained that an evil and very powerful sorceress had cast a spell on her and if anyone outside of the forest learned of her plight she would instantly turn into a raven and be trapped in the cage forever. A tear trickled down her cheek as she sent Tadleigh away with a promise never to speak of their encounter."

"So he just left her in the cage?"

"At first. He went back to his village and tried very hard not to speak of what he'd seen in the forest. But Tadleigh couldn't hold his tongue and he told the miller, swearing the old man to secrecy. The miller told the bootmaker and the bootmaker told the blacksmith, and before long, a group had gathered at the forest's edge to rescue the princess, each person vying for her favor and the reward. Tadleigh frantically tried to explain that he'd made the story up, but this time, no one would believe him. The townsfolk hurried into the forest and found the golden cage. With the help of many strong men, they lowered it and broke the lock with a woodsman's axe."

"And the princess was rescued?"

"Not exactly. The moment the princess stepped out of the cage, she turned into an old crone with stringy black hair and a hooked nose that looked like a raven's beak. She laughed, a loud cackle that echoed through the forest, shouting that she knew all along that Tadleigh couldn't hold his tongue. She waved her arms and chanted a spell and all the townspeople turned to squawking ravens. Tadleigh was stunned to find all his friends turned to ugly black birds. Then the crone turned to him and pointed a gnarled finger. 'Beauty is not always what it seems,' she told him. She disappeared into the depths of the forest, never to be seen again."

"What happened to Tadleigh?"

"He walked back to the village all alone, knowing that he'd been tricked by his own tongue. And from then on, until the day he died, Tadleigh had no one to tell his stories to but the ravens in the trees."

"So the moral of the story is, know when to keep your mouth shut."

He stared over at her and smiled. "The moral of the story is, princesses are not always what they seem. And beauty can hide a multitude of evils."

With that, he pushed himself off the bed, leaving Amy to ponder the story further. She couldn't miss the parallels to her own story. When he'd closed the door behind him, Amy paged through the notebook, looking for the story of Tadleigh and the princess, but couldn't find it. Then she realized that the story probably hadn't existed until just a few minutes ago.

She wasn't what she appeared to be, this princess who he'd rescued from the Longliner Tap. But if she told him the truth, would she still be his princess? Or would her lies turn her into the crone who left poor Tadleigh to live his life alone?

"DID YOU TYPE up those notes?" Brendan asked, shuffling through a mess of papers on the galley table. He'd rifled though the file folder twice looking for a piece of paper he knew he'd put there. But it was nowhere to be found.

He and Amy had been working all day, editing and rewriting, arguing over silly little points and drinking entirely too much coffee. "I told you I needed those notes tonight."

Amy glanced up from the computer and sighed impatiently. "I'm still trying to decipher your handwriting. You should have taken your tape recorder."

"Some people don't like to talk with a tape recorder running," Brendan muttered, grabbing another folder. "It makes them inhibited. How long until you're finished? I want to get this chapter cleaned up by the end of the night."

She stared at him from across the cabin, her expression tight. "Why don't you go out for a walk?"

"I don't want to take a walk," he snapped. He'd been on edge all day, his mind occupied with thoughts of Amy, instead of his writing. The longer she lived on the boat, the harder it was to concentrate. Again and again, he'd told himself that getting involved with her would be a colossal mistake. But avoiding involvement was taking so much energy that it was leaving him exhausted and short-tempered. Something was going to happen—either he was going to make love to her or he was going to fire her. Whatever it was, it was going to happen soon.

He stole another glance at her, his gaze dropping to her outfit. Amy had worn some odd things, but he had to believe she'd chosen her clothes this morning with the intention of driving him crazy. She wore a short little plaid skirt and a turtleneck sweater that hugged her slender frame. She also had on kneesocks that made her look like every boy's schoolgirl fantasy.

"Take a nap," Amy suggested, "or drink a beer or knit a sweater. Just stop bothering me. I'm trying to finish typing in these changes."

Brendan crossed his arms over his chest and stared at her stubbornly. "It's my job to bug you. I'm your boss."

"And it's my job to tell you when you need to chill," she yelled. She shut the laptop and crawled off the sofa berth, then crossed the main cabin to the galley table. Without a word, she began to pick up his papers and stack them into neat little piles. Then she reached for his computer and turned it off. "We're done for the evening," she said.

"We are not," he said, flipping it back on. "We're done when I say we're done."

Amy hitched her hands on her hips. "Are you under the impression that you call the shots here?"

"I am, and I do."

"Well, tough. I'm officially on strike then."

"You can't go on strike," Brendan countered. "If you go on strike, I'll fire you." He paused. "You're fired."

"You can't fire me," she shot back, the color rising in her cheeks. "You don't pay me enough to fire me. I'll quit first." She crossed to the galley, reached into the icebox and pulled out a bottle of wine. "I quit. Now, why don't we have a nice glass of wine? And after we do, you can beg me to come back to work for you. Maybe you can even offer me a raise?"

Brendan ground his teeth. She had an uncanny way of putting him in his place, especially when he was acting like a jerk. But he was too frustrated to let it go. "How do you know I'm going to ask you back?"

"Because I'm the best assistant you've ever had," she said, yanking out the cork.

"You're the *only* assistant I've ever had. And I did just fine without you."

"You did? All right, you did." She reached over to a pile of index cards sitting on the counter then tossed them up in the air. They scattered all over the floor of the cabin. "That's about how well your notes were organized when I started." She picked up a box of microcassettes and one by one, threw them around the room. Then she walked over to the laptop and rubbed the top of it. "I wonder what would happen to all the notes I typed up if I dropped this computer in the harbor?"

Brendan crossed the cabin in three long strides, holding out his hand. "I wouldn't do that if I were you."

"Oh, no? Then I'd apologize for not appreciating the true value of my contributions."

"I don't owe you an apology. You're the one who started all this."

She stared at him for a long moment, then cursed softly. "You're right," she said. "This isn't working out. Maybe it would be best if I quit." With that, she turned, grabbed her jacket from a hook on the bulkhead and walked to the door to the deck. "I'll go see if they'll give me my job back at the Longliner."

At first, Brendan thought she was just baiting him. But as she stepped up on deck, panic set in. Amy was obstinate enough to go through with this. He cursed softly, then followed her, catching up with her just as she was stepping off the boat. He grabbed her wrist. "I do appreciate you," he murmured.

She slowly turned, her eyebrow arched inquisitively. "What did you say? I didn't hear you."

"I do appreciate you," he repeated, pulling her back onto the deck.

"More than you can possibly say?" she asked.

"I'm the writer here," he said, slipping his arms around her waist and leaning closer, unable to resist her a moment longer. "Let me write my own dialogue."

He didn't really think before kissing her. If he had, he might have stopped himself. But Brendan was past the point of common sense, past the point of rational thought. He had given himself over to instinct and instinct told him to kiss Amy and not stop until he'd had enough.

The moment his mouth touched hers, he marveled how good a simple kiss could feel, how the taste of her seeped into his bloodstream and washed away the last trace of control that he possessed. All his excuses for keeping his distance seemed silly at best. This wasn't a typical boss-employee relationship and it never had been. He and Amy had been destined to share this from the start and he'd delayed longer than any sensible man would have.

Brendan's hands drifted up to her face and furrowed through her hair, tipping her head as his lips traced a line from her jaw to the soft skin beneath her ear. She made no attempt to resist and when he drew back and gazed down at her face, he saw a smile curling the corners of her mouth.

"We should go back inside," he said, smoothing his palm over her cheek.

"No," she murmured. She pushed her hands inside his jacket. "I'm warm." She paused. "You're warm. Let's stay out here."

Brendan followed her lead and slid his hands inside her jacket. He slipped his fingers under the bottom of her sweater, touching bare skin. Maybe this was best, out in the cold. They couldn't possibly tear each other's clothes off and give in to their passions. But Amy didn't seem to notice their surroundings. She pressed her forehead against his chest and slowly began to unbutton his flannel shirt.

"What are you doing?" he asked with a low groan.

"Keeping warm." She pressed her lips against his skin, then moved over and circled his nipple with her tongue. The instant she pulled away, the cold hit his damp skin, sending an exquisite mixture of pleasure and pain skittering through his body.

Brendan had always considered himself fairly adventurous when it came to passionate encounters, but the notion of making love to Amy beneath the winter sky was beyond anything he'd ever considered. He'd known from the start that Amy wasn't a traditional girl. Why had he expected this encounter to be any different? As she bent down and circled his belly button with her tongue, Brendan furrowed his hands through her hair and moaned softly.

Strange new sensations shot through him as he drew her up, her tongue tracing a line to his collarbone. He captured her mouth again, desperate to share at least that warmth with her. The taste of Amy was addictive. He couldn't go too long without it. But her touch was becoming even more so and when she reached for the button of his jeans, Brendan knew exactly where they were headed—and he wasn't about to stop her.

Slowly, he pushed his hands up beneath her sweater to cup her breasts in his palms. As he teased at her nipples with his thumbs, she shuddered, her hands beginning to tremble. Her nipples grew hard beneath his touch. Brendan drew back and stared down into her beautiful face. "You are cold," he murmured.

"No," she said, sliding his zipper down. "I'm very warm."

With that denial, Brendan knew what she wanted and he became desperate to give it to her. He dispensed with the clasp on her bra and explored her curves with his fingers. He couldn't look at her body the way he would if they were inside, but his imagination was making up for it. It was almost more tantalizing seducing her fully dressed than completely naked.

Brendan grabbed her waist and pressed her back against the outside of the main cabin. The light spilling out of the cabin illuminated one side of her face, the other lost in shadow. "You're so beautiful," he murmured, bending lower to slide his hands beneath her skirt.

He wasn't sure what it was about the little skirt, only that he would have chosen it over any black lingerie when it came to sexy attire. He smoothed his hands over her backside, her curves made for his hands. The wind fluttered at her skirt and Brendan wondered how she could stand the cold. But she seemed oblivious to it, moaning softly as he touched her, ran his hands beneath her panties.

Suddenly, a frigid breeze buffeted them both. But rather than cooling their desire, the wind seemed to make it more intense. Amy reached down and ran her hand over his belly, then brushed against the hard ridge of his erection beneath his jeans. The instant she touched him, Brendan sucked in a sharp breath. When she slipped her fingers beneath his boxers, when her cold hand met his hot sex, another jolt of desire slammed through him.

Slowly, she caressed him, the heat radiating through his body then dissipating in the cold air. He barely noticed the temperature now and in some ways he was grateful for it. It heightened his senses, kept his head clear. And without it, her touch might bring him to the edge too quickly.

He braced his hands on either side of her head as she stroked him, losing himself in the waves of sensation.

Brendan knew he wouldn't last forever. He wanted to be inside her, feeling her heat wrapped around him.

As if she could read his desire, she slowed her pace. "I think we might need...something," she murmured.

"A blanket?" he teased. He reached into his back pocket, took out his wallet and pulled out a foil packet. His fingers were beginning to go numb with the cold, but he tore the foil open, then handed it to her. Amy smoothed the condom over him, the simple act causing him to told his breath and try to concentrate on other things.

Then she looked up at him. "Make love to me," she murmured.

"Not until you tell me," he murmured.

"Tell you what?"

Brendan took a ragged breath and bent closer, his mouth pressed against her ear. "Tell me there's no one else."

"There's no one else," Amy whispered with a soft sigh.

Their course set, Brendan gave up the last shred of his control. He slid down, grabbed Amy and picked her up, wrapping her legs around his waist. His erection pressed at the damp fabric of her panties, probing toward the warmth, the incredible warmth. He reached down and pushed aside the fabric, then gently, slowly entered her.

The heat was exquisite and for a moment, he stilled, his mind spinning, his heart pounding, his breath clouding in front of his face. She wriggled against him, sliding down until he was buried inside her. Brendan tried to draw another breath but it was nearly impossible. Every nerve of his being was electrified, crackling until the pleasure was too much to deny.

She murmured his name and he began to move, pushing her back against the bulkhead. Each thrust sent him closer to the edge, closer to perfection. He'd never experienced anything like Amy and the absolute need to possess her, the undeniable push toward release. But he didn't want just her body, he wanted something more, something beyond the physical.

Their rhythm increased and Brendan lost touch with reality. Every nerve, every thought was focused on the spot where they were joined. Her breath came in tiny gasps and he shifted slightly, increasing her pleasure. She moaned and cried out, arching against the wall as he drove harder. He knew she was near.

And then, like water breaking over the bow, she let go, sinking against him with a sigh and a shudder and a wave of contractions. He thrust once more, then followed her into the abyss, caught in a whirlpool of sensation. He'd worked so hard to keep himself from loving her, but at this moment, Brendan realized that it all was just destiny at work. His being in the bar that night, her needing a job and a place to stay. Their joining beneath the clear winter sky.

At first it had seemed outlandish, making love in the cold. But now he knew it was a memory that would remain vivid in his mind—cold hands and warm mouths, the rigging clanking above their heads, the water sloshing against the hull and swells of exquisite pleasure.

He buried his face in the curve of her neck and leaned into her, not willing to break their intimate connection. But without movement, the cold began to seep through his clothes.

"We have to go inside," she murmured, kissing his neck. "I'm freezing."

"This seems to be a theme with you," he teased. "You get cold and I have to find a way to warm you up."

Amy giggled, running her fingers through his hair. "I like this method," she said, brushing a lock from his forehead.

"Me, too," he replied, laughing softly at their predicament. Holding onto her, he stepped back, then stumbled to the hatch. Amy cried out as he nearly lost his balance, wrapping her arms and legs more tightly around him. When he got inside, he slammed the hatch shut, then carried her to his berth. She wouldn't be sleeping in the crew cabin anymore. She'd share his bed from now on.

another, but neither of them found the right words to say. Finally he took a deep breath. "When will we—" she began.

"When are we—" he said simultaneously. Embarrassed, Amy laughed.

"You go first," he said. "I was going to ask you the—

5

"WE SHOULD GET UP," Amy murmured, rolling over on top of Brendan and straddling his hips, her breasts pressed to his chest. She could feel his heart beating slow and strong. A moan rumbled in his chest.

The moment they'd tumbled onto his bed last night, they'd tossed aside their clothes, anxious to experience new pleasures in each other's body. And they had, making love until the early morning hours. In the end, they'd fallen asleep, exhausted and completely sated, both a bit shocked by the depth of their desire.

She pressed a kiss to the smooth skin below his collarbone. "It's already past noon and you wanted to get the first half of your book polished before we started working on chapter ten."

"You're a stern taskmaster," he teased, playfully nipping at her ear. "And you make me do things that I don't want to do." He chuckled. "Very naughty things."

"I knew you were a prude," she said.

He slowly stroked her hair, his expression turning serious. "You know, you're very good at what you do, Amy."

Amy's face warmed with a blush. "I haven't had that much experience with men," she murmured.

"No, I don't mean sex," Brendan said. "Although

you're very good at that, too. I mean your work with my book. The help you're giving me. After we're through, I think you should consider getting a job with a publishing house. You could start as a reader. With your talent, it wouldn't take you long to move up." He looked deeply into her eyes as he distractedly smoothed her hair with his fingers. "You could be an editor in no time. I could put in a good word with my publisher. Maybe write you a letter of recommendation."

"You really think I'd be good?" Amy asked, warmed by his compliment. Her parents had insisted the only job she was qualified for was that of society wife, married to a man smart enough to handle her money and devoted enough to provide them with grandchildren.

Brendan nodded. "Yeah, I do."

She sighed. "I'll think about it. I'd like to live in New York."

"New York?"

She pushed up and tossed her hair out of her eyes. "I can't stay here forever. You'll only have a job for me for another few weeks at the most. Then I'll have to move on." Amy reached out and traced the furrows from his forehead. "Don't worry about me. I like working for you, Brendan. I've learned a lot."

"Working *with* me," he said.

"With you," she repeated. "It's the best job I've ever had." With a sudden realization, she looked down at her naked breasts and giggled. Amy grabbed the comforter and pulled it around her. "I forgot I was in bed with the boss." She winced. "What we did last night—and this morning…. It was all right, wasn't it?"

Brendan reached up and cupped her cheek in his hand. "What are you asking? Are you asking if I enjoyed it? Or are you asking if I'm sorry it happened?"

"I'm asking if it will change things between us," Amy said.

Brendan grabbed her around the waist and rolled her beneath him. Bracing himself on his elbow, he toyed with a strand of her hair as he studied her face. "I think it already has." He dipped down and stole a kiss, then grinned. "And yes, I enjoyed it, and no, I'm not sorry. I hope it happens again. Soon. But not in the next five minutes or so. Does that answer all your questions?"

She nodded, then drew a shaky breath. "You know, this doesn't have to mean anything," she murmured. "We got carried away last night. But I don't expect anything from you because of it."

Brendan frowned. "What are you saying?"

Amy forced a smile. This was not how she wanted to begin the day, with a convoluted explanation of her feelings toward him. Or a half-hearted attempt to discern his feelings about her.

She didn't really know how she felt. On one hand, she knew a relationship with any man was impossible right now. But on the other hand, she couldn't help but be a tiny bit in love with Brendan. Well, maybe more than just a tiny bit. He made it so easy to care for him. "I'm just saying that I don't expect any marriage proposals. We're here, together, and what we shared was wonderful. But it doesn't have to mean any more than it does. It's nice for now, but it's not forever."

Brendan sat up in bed and stared at her for a long

moment. He opened his mouth as if to contradict her, then shook his head. "No, you're right. It doesn't have to mean anything."

"It's just that I can't make any promises," she continued. "But if I could, you'd be the first one I'd make promises to."

He cursed softly. "I don't need promises." Brendan crawled out of bed and searched the cabin for his jeans. "I'm going to make some coffee." Her gaze took in his body, from his broad shoulders to his narrow waist and hips, to his perfect backside. A little shiver skittered through her and she pulled the comforter more tightly around her.

Brendan found his jeans on the floor near the door, then tugged them on, not bothering with boxer shorts. Amy silently watched him from the bed, watched the tense muscles of his shoulders and the grim set of his mouth. He was angry with her. Something she'd said had upset him. But she'd said nothing that he shouldn't have been thinking himself. They barely knew each other, and though they shared an undeniable physical desire, this couldn't possibly lead to something more serious. She drew another shaky breath. Or could it?

Had their night together been more than just a physical release? Though she'd tried hard to control her feelings for him, she'd never once thought that he might have deeper feelings for her. But how could he? He didn't even know who she was.

He reached out for the door, then paused and turned back to her. "You know, I don't really care about your past," he said. "And since we met, I haven't even thought about my past. But if you can't trust me with the truth, Amy, then we shouldn't be doing this."

"Working together?"

"No, sleeping together."

She felt a warm blush work its way up her cheeks. "If you don't want to—"

"Damn it, I do want to. What I don't want is to make love with a stranger. Believe me, this is all new territory here. With any other woman, I'd be happy to keep my distance. But you're..." Amy waited for him to finish his sentence, but all she got was a shake of his head. "Maybe we got carried away last night, but it's not going to happen again. Not until you tell me who you are and what you're running from."

"And what if you don't like what I tell you?"

He raked his fingers through his hair. "What is it? Are you an escaped convict? Did you bilk an old lady out of her life savings? Did you pull an armored car heist?" He paused, cursing beneath his breath. "Are you married? I mean, what could be so bad that you can't tell me?"

"No," Amy said. "I'm not married. And I haven't done anything wrong. I just hoped that you'd care about me for who I am. Not who I was."

Brendan let out a tightly held breath. "I do," he said. "Why do you think I pulled you out of the Longliner? Or saved you from hypothermia?" He sat down on the edge of the berth and took her hand. "I swear, it won't make a difference. Just tell me."

"You don't know that," she said. "It always makes a difference. Believe me, it does."

"When you're ready to talk, I'll be ready to listen."

With that, he leaned forward and brushed a quick kiss across her lips, then stood and walked out the door.

As the door clicked shut behind him Amy flopped back on the bed, throwing her arm over her eyes. Why not tell him the truth? It wasn't as if she'd done something bad. She was rich, her family had tons of money. And until six months ago, she had been engaged. For all she knew, she was still technically engaged since she hadn't officially broken things off with Craig.

But over the past six months, Amy had learned one hard lesson. The only person she could trust was herself. Few people would really understand why she'd run away. She had needed to find out who she was, away from her family and their money. And in six months, she'd made a lot of progress. But there was still work to be done. She still had to figure out how to make a living. Though her grandmother's trust would pay the rent, she didn't want to spend the rest of her life in worthless pursuits. She wanted a good job with a bright future.

Amy rolled over on her stomach and smoothed her hands over her pillow. Her mind wandered back to the night before, the incredible passion she'd shared with Brendan. She'd expected the experience to be good, but she hadn't expected it to change the way she thought about herself.

After Craig, she'd grown wary, certain that falling in love would mean having to compromise who she was. She'd spent the first part of her life being the daughter of Avery Aldrich Sloane. She didn't want to spend the rest of it being known as the wife of some powerful man. Brendan had shown her the depths of her passion. He'd opened a door and let her look more clearly at the woman she was.

Even if they didn't have a future together, she had to find a way to thank him for all he'd done for her. Making mad, passionate love to him for the rest of the day seemed like the best way. But she wanted something more tangible, some part of herself that she could leave with him after she was gone.

Her gaze fell on the spiral notebook stuffed among the magazines on the shelf above his berth. Amy reached over and pulled it out, then slowly flipped through it. An idea began to grow in her mind and by the time she paged to the last Mighty Quinn story, she knew what she could do. She'd make him a Christmas present, something that came from her heart... something meant to touch his.

Whether they were together for this Christmas or they parted ways in the days before, he'd always have something to remind him of her.

BRENDAN HEFTED the bags of groceries up as he walked along the wharf near where *The Mighty Quinn* was moored. He'd asked Amy to do the grocery shopping but she'd insisted that she had other more important things to do. She'd seemed anxious to get rid of him and in truth, he was anxious to put a little space between them. He'd spent nearly the entire afternoon running meaningless errands—taking his car to the car wash, shopping at a local discount store for a few new T-shirts, stopping by his favorite restaurant for a piece of apple pie.

He knew as soon as he went back to the boat his

mind would be plagued with thoughts of the previous evening. Even now, images flashed in his brain, taking him right back to their incredible encounter on the deck of *The Mighty Quinn*. No matter how hard he tried, Brendan couldn't explain away the need, the overwhelming physical release or the undeniable emotional attachment that had grown between them.

He'd tried to rationalize the connection between the pleasures of the flesh and the desires of the heart. But even without a sexual component, he still cared about Amy—more than he'd ever cared about a woman before. Maybe it was because he felt responsible for her. He'd saved her from the bar fight, given her a job and a place to live, invited her into his life.

There was more to it than that. The instant she'd mentioned moving to New York, his mind had formed a plan. He could live in New York. Why not? His home base had always been *The Mighty Quinn*, but why not an apartment in the city. He'd instantly put aside his connections to Boston, his commitment to a commitmentless life and his determination not to follow in Conor and Dylan's footsteps. The mere thought of being away from Amy for even a day or two was too difficult to imagine.

Brendan stopped walking, then cursed softly. "If you're not completely in love now, then you're sure falling fast and hard, boyo."

But what could he do? He couldn't just ignore his feelings for her. Though Conor didn't approve and Dylan probably would side with him, Brendan's choice in the matter wasn't really a choice at all. She'd stumbled into his life and weaseled her way into his heart. At every turn, she'd come to him for help, whether it was to rescue her from a drunk or to warm her body in his bed. He'd come to enjoy the role he played in her life as the protector and he couldn't see her getting along without him. Hell, she'd probably freeze to death at the first opportunity.

He'd made a promise to her as they lay in bed, vowing that they wouldn't sleep together again until she told him the truth about herself. But Brendan realized that the truth really didn't matter. It was as if his life—and hers—had begun the moment their eyes met across the smoky interior of the Longliner.

As he turned to head down the pier to *The Mighty Quinn*, a man in a dark trench coat stepped out from behind a lamppost. Though he showed no signs of aggression, Brendan knew the man had intended to surprise him. His instincts on alert, he readied himself to swing the bags of groceries at the guy's head. There were some nice canned goods inside that would put a decent dent in his noggin.

"Do you live on one of these boats?" the man asked, his eyes watching Brendan with a shrewd squint.

On any other day, from any other person, the question would seem quite innocent. But this man wasn't the usual type that hung around the waterfront. He wasn't a fisherman and he wasn't a sailor. In truth, he looked like some underworld figure with a bad haircut. "Why do you want to know?" Brendan asked.

The guy reached into his pocket and produced a small photo of a smiling young couple. "I'm looking for this woman. She's been seen in the area recently."

Brendan set the groceries down at his feet and took

the photo from the man's hand. At first, he barely glanced at it. But then, he took a closer look, at the pretty brunette with the wide eyes and the impish smile. Bleach the hair, add outrageous earrings and makeup and you'd have Amy Aldrich. "Who is she?" Brendan asked.

"I can't tell you," the man said. "Have you seen her? There is a reward for information regarding her whereabouts."

"Who's the guy? Her husband?" In truth, Brendan didn't want to hear the answer. He'd already decided it didn't make a difference.

"Her fiancé," the man answered.

Brendan stared at the picture for a long moment, not sure whether the news was good or bad. She wasn't married, she was just engaged. But that meant that there was a loving fiancé waiting for her—someone who might want her back for all the right reasons.

The man smiling out from the photo looked nothing like the type of man the Amy he knew might be attracted to. Dressed in a sleek business suit, he looked like he'd just stepped off the pages of some corporate report, all clean-cut and conservative. Brendan looked again at the picture of Amy, just to make sure it was really her, then gave a casual shrug. "I've never seen her before."

"She might have blond hair now," the guy said. "And we think she might know someone on one of these boats."

Brendan smiled apologetically. "There aren't too many people around here this time of year. In a few more weeks most of the recreational boats will be hauled out for the winter." He paused. "But there was a guy who was living on a boat moored just down there." Brendan pointed past *The Mighty Quinn*. "If I remember right, he had a blonde with him. Petite, maybe five four. And young. They took off early yesterday morning. I think he might have been heading down the coast to warmer weather."

"Do you know where?"

"He was always talking about Baltimore, but I'm not sure if that's where he was going."

"Thanks," the man said.

Brendan held tight to the picture. "Do you mind if I keep this. In case they come back?" He shrugged. "I could use the reward money."

The man seemed surprised, then nodded curtly. He withdrew a pen from his jacket pocket and scribbled a phone number on the back. "My cell phone. You can reach me any time."

"How much is the reward?" Brendan asked.

"Two hundred and fifty thousand," the man said.

Brendan quelled a gasp of surprise and attempted to appear indifferent. A quarter of a million dollars for the whereabouts of Amy Aldrich? "That's a lot of money."

"Her family just wants to make sure she's all right." With that, the man turned on his heel and started off down the dock. He'd been so stone-faced that Brendan wasn't sure he'd fooled him. But as he watched him walk off, Brendan reevaluated their conversation. Was he the guy who had caused Amy to jump in the freezing water? Brendan fought the urge to follow him and give him a well-aimed puck in the gob.

Instead, he shook his head and picked up his groceries. So much for his distaste for the manly art of fisticuffs. When it came to Amy, he felt like punching the guy in the trench coat, the drunk at the bar and most especially, the uptight, buttondown creep in the photograph.

When he got up on deck he took a long look across the waterfront, searching for the man who was searching for Amy. But he was nowhere to be found. Brendan stepped through the hatch and found the main cabin empty. "Amy?"

He set the groceries down and walked forward, looking into her cabin and his. The boat was silent. His mind immediately went to the man outside. If Amy was off the boat, then there was every chance he'd run into her on the way back. Brendan cursed softly and began to pace the length of the main cabin. Where would she have gone? She'd sent him out for groceries with some excuse about having something important to do.

Brendan's breath froze, then he hurried back to her cabin, expecting to see all her belongings gone. But clothes were still scattered over her berth and her suitcase was tossed on the bunk above. He headed back toward the hatch, determined to go out and find her. She didn't have a car, so she couldn't have gone far. But just as he was opening the hatch door, she appeared.

"Where the hell have you been?" Brendan asked.

The wide smile faded from her face, replaced by a frown. "I was out," she said.

He reached into his pocket, ready to wave the photo under her nose and demand an explanation. Or maybe he'd throw his meeting with the guy in the trench coat at her. But a cooler mind prevailed and Brendan stepped away from the hatch, allowing her to pass.

"What's wrong with you?" she asked, giving him a look as she climbed down the stairs.

"Nothing," he said. "When I found you gone, I thought maybe you'd fallen in and drowned."

Amy shrugged off her jacket and tossed it on the sofa berth, then grabbed the laptop and sat down at the galley table. She flipped it open and waited for the program to load, tapping her fingers impatiently on the table.

"Aren't you going to tell me where you were?" Brendan asked.

"What are you, my mother?" she murmured. She reached in her pocket and pulled out a sheaf of papers, then smoothed them out beside the computer. A few moments later, she began to type, her fingers flying over the keys. When he opened his mouth to speak, she held up her hand to stop him. "Just one second," she said. She returned to her typing, ignoring him for a full five minutes.

Brendan slipped out of his own jacket then returned to the counter to unpack the groceries. By the time he was done, she had stopped typing but was still staring at the screen. "There," she murmured, "I think I got it."

"Got what? Tomorrow's grocery list?"

"The interview," she said.

Brendan froze as he was reaching into the bag to pull out a carton of orange juice.

"A job interview?"

Amy smiled, then hopped up from the table. "No, silly," she said, wrapping her arms around his neck and giving him a quick kiss on the cheek. "The interview with Denise Antonini, the wife of Captain John Antonini, that swordfishing captain whose boat was lost at sea."

"You got me an interview with her?" Brendan asked in disbelief. "How did you do that? She didn't want to talk to me. I've been calling her every few weeks for the last four months."

"I didn't exactly get *you* an interview," she said. "Though that's why I called her originally, to try to convince her to talk to you. I mean, that's what an assistant is supposed to do, right? She still refused and then we got talking and before I knew it, she was pouring her heart out to me. I was scribbling notes as fast as I could, trying to keep up with what she was telling me. Then she said, let's meet for lunch at the Longliner and we did. I tried to think of all the questions you'd ask." Amy tipped her head back and laughed, then turned and grabbed her papers from the table. "It's all here. This is what you need to make that chapter work."

Brendan stared down at her notes. "You shouldn't have done that," he murmured, stepping away.

She seemed stunned by his reply. "Why? You said you needed the interview and I got it for you."

"You got it for *you*," Brendan said. "I have no idea what this woman told you. I can't quote her because I didn't interview her. And now that she's talked to you, she isn't going to want to talk to me."

"But I have everything right here," Amy said. "And

I can remember almost every word of our conversation."

"Unless you can remember every single word of every single sentence, I can't use it."

Amy frowned, then hit him with the papers. "You're just being stubborn. You're mad because I got the interview when you couldn't!"

Brendan opened his mouth to snap back at her, but then noticed the expression on her face. She'd seemed so excited when she told him her news. Now she looked hurt and insulted. And he was the cause. He cursed himself inwardly, then reached out and took her hand. He wasn't angry about the interview. And he could use what she'd learned. He'd just been so worried to find her gone that he'd taken it out on her.

"I'm sorry," Brendan said, reaching out to slip his hands around her waist.

"You should be," she muttered.

"I couldn't have gotten that interview. She wasn't going to talk to me, but she talked to you."

A tiny smile curled the corners of her mouth. "Then it's all right?"

He bent his head and kissed her temple. "It's great." He pulled back and looked down into her eyes. "Since you got the interview, then we'd better get to work on putting it in the book."

Amy pulled out of his embrace and hurried to the table. "I'm ready whenever you are," she said, her hands poised above the keyboard.

Brendan stared at her for a long moment, feeling his heart beating a little faster in his chest. It hadn't come as a huge revelation, with bells ringing and fireworks popping. It hadn't even come as a heart-stopping realization. It had come in one single second, in the blink of an eye, when he looked down into Amy's face and realized that he had the capacity to hurt her.

In that single moment, Brendan knew he never wanted to hurt her again. In that moment, he knew one other thing beyond any doubt. He was in love with Amy Aldrich and nothing he did would make those feelings go away.

"SO WHERE IS SHE?" Conor asked. He looked around the main cabin of *The Mighty Quinn*.

Brendan glanced up from the galley counter as he poured his brother a cup of coffee. "She's not here. She walked into town to do some shopping. She'll be back in a little while," he said. "Why are you so anxious to meet her? I didn't think you approved."

"So, did she take her purse with her?" Conor asked.

Brendan frowned. "Why the hell do you care?"

"Because, she's not here. We should search her cabin and see what we can find. Take a look inside her purse. The clues you gave me the other day weren't much to go on. Give me something she touched and I'll take it in and lift some prints. If she has a record, we'll have her fingerprints on file."

"No," Brendan said.

"There has to be something with her prints on it," Conor insisted.

"That's not what I mean." He pointed to the table. "Sit."

Conor did as he was told. Brendan grabbed a cup of coffee for himself, then leaned up against the edge of the counter. He should have known the moment Conor hopped onboard *The Mighty Quinn* that he wasn't here for a social call. Though his brother often stopped by for a visit whenever he had the time, he usually called Brendan from a nearby bar, inviting him out for beer or two. It was clear that he'd come to Gloucester to do one thing and one thing only—check out Amy Aldrich.

"I don't want you to run her fingerprints," Brendan said. "It's not necessary."

"Then she told you who she was?"

Brendan shook his head. "No. But it doesn't matter. I don't care about her past."

Conor rolled his eyes and shook his head, the way his always had when his little brothers didn't want to listen. "You're making a mistake."

"Maybe I am," Brendan said. He paused, unsure of how he wanted to say the words. In the end, he came right out and said them. "I think I'm in love with her, Con."

His older brother groaned, then rubbed his forehead as if to smooth out the lines of worry that had been there since he'd arrived. "You can't be serious."

"I wish I wasn't. I never expected this, but I'm about as serious as I can be considering the circumstances. I don't care who she is or where she came from. Or what she's done in the past. We've got something special going and digging up the past isn't going to make it any better."

Conor wrapped his hands around his coffee mug

and stared into the steaming brew. "So tell me, what you do know?" He glanced up. "Just to reassure me."

Brendan walked over to his computer case and pulled a folder out of the front pocket. He handed Conor the picture that the man on the dock had given him. "That's her," Brendan said. "Some guy was here yesterday looking for her. He looked like a private detective. He said the man in the photo is her fiancé."

"This is her?" Conor frowned. "She doesn't look like a criminal."

"She's not. At least I don't think she is. The guy said her family is looking for her. They're offering a quarter of a million for any information leading to her location."

"A quarter of a million dollars?"

"No, a quarter of a million hamburgers," Brendan replied.

"Man, she must be someone pretty important to offer that kind of dough." He flipped the picture over. "What's this?"

"The detective's phone number. He said if I saw her, I should call him."

Conor stared at the picture for a long time. "Do you mind if I take this?"

"For what?"

"I'm just going to do some checking. If you won't let me search her cabin or take her fingerprints, let me find out what this detective knows and I'll get back to you."

"So you think she's okay?" Brendan asked, anxious for reassurance.

Conor slipped the photo inside his jacket pocket.

"My guess? Either she's a bank teller who embezzled a few million and is now on the run and the bit about the family and the reward is just garbage. Or she's the daughter of a rich guy who wants his baby girl back."

"But if she's the daughter of some rich guy, why did she run away? Her father can't run her life. She's an adult."

Conor's brow rose. "Are you sure? Are you sure she isn't seventeen posing as twenty-seven? Have you ever asked her how old she is?"

Brendan stared at his brother, unable to speak. "Oh, God," he finally said, his heart leaping up to his throat. "I never thought of that. I just assumed. I was worried about her being married. I mean, she doesn't act like a teenager."

"They never do," Conor said.

"No way," Brendan said. "She's too smart. She knows too much. She's—" He swallowed hard, all the ramifications of that possibility rushing through his brain. He closed his eyes and tried to put order to his thoughts. No, she had to be at least twenty-three or twenty-four. "She has a fiancé. She couldn't be a teenager."

"Still, it's lucky you haven't slept with her," Conor said.

Brendan's eyes snapped open. "Yeah," he replied with a weak laugh. "Very lucky."

Footsteps sounded on the deck above their heads and they both turned to see the hatch open and Amy appear. She carried two shopping bags and an open can of soda. Brendan breathed a silent sigh of relief. He was still worried about the detective hanging around, not sure that he'd believed the story about Amy and the boat to Baltimore.

He stepped up to the hatch and grabbed the shopping bags, then helped her down the stairs. When she reached the bottom, she smiled at Conor, then looked to Brendan for an introduction. "Hi," she said.

"Hi," Brendan replied.

Amy frowned, then crossed the cabin to the table. She held out her hand. "I'm Amy Aldrich, Brendan's assistant. You must be one of his brothers. You look alike."

Brendan watched as Conor took in the new arrival. An expression of what Brendan could only call appreciation suffused his brother's face. If he wasn't mistaken, his brother had just been charmed. "I'm Conor Quinn," he said.

Amy shook his hand. "It's so nice to meet you. I've heard all about the Quinns. Brendan's been telling me tales about your ancestors."

"He has." A smile quirked the corners of Conor's mouth. "He hasn't told us anything about you."

Brendan stepped to her side and slipped his arm around her shoulders. "Conor is always full of questions. It's in his nature. He was just asking me how old you were and I wasn't able to tell him."

Amy looked back and forth between the two of them, frowning. "I don't think I've ever mentioned it."

"Ah," Brendan said. "That's why I didn't know." He paused. "So, how old are you?"

Amy blinked, clearly confused. "I'm twenty-five," she said.

Brendan smiled and sent his brother an "I-told-you-so" glare. "Really? Well, that's interesting. Nice to know."

"It is?" she asked. "Why?"

"Because, now Conor has his answer. And he'll be leaving, won't you, Conor."

Amy shook her head. "But—but we haven't had a chance to get to know each other," she said. "We could at least invite him to stay for dinner." She turned to Conor. "You will stay, won't you? I'm not much of a cook, but we could send out for a pizza. Please stay."

Brendan gave her shoulders a squeeze. "Conor has to get back to work. He's a cop. In Boston. Did I tell you that?"

He felt Amy stiffen slightly and her smile faded by a few degrees. "No, you didn't mention that." She drew a deep breath. "Well then, it was a pleasure meeting you. I hope you'll stop by again soon."

Conor slowly stood and walked to the stairs. "It was nice to meet you, too, Amy." He turned to Brendan. "I'll call you with that information we discussed."

A few seconds later, Conor stepped through the hatch and closed the door behind him. Amy's gaze was fixed on the spot where he last stood. "I don't think your brother likes me," she murmured.

"He doesn't know you," Brendan said.

Amy shook her head. "No, I'm very intuitive, and he doesn't like me."

Brendan slipped his arm around her shoulders and

gently pulled her closer. "Conor doesn't matter," he murmured. "I like you and that's what matters."

Amy turned to him, her expression suddenly bright and her smile wide. She pushed up on her toes and brushed a quick kiss across his mouth, leaving him wanting more. "I like you, too," she said.

6

AMY WOKE to the sounds she'd grown used to in the past week—the water lapping at the sides of the boat, the clank of rigging above her head and the raucous sound of seagulls, willing to brave the early December cold for a fish breakfast. She stretched her arms out over her head and snuggled back beneath the blankets on Brendan's berth. "While the cat's away, the mice will play," she murmured, smiling contentedly.

Brendan had left yesterday afternoon for a meeting in New York. He'd written a whole list of things for Amy to do while he was gone, but after she'd dropped him off at the train station, she'd taken off for a day of shopping. Two hundred dollars cash was a windfall to her, considering she didn't have to pay for rent or food.

So she went to the local discount store and bought three sweaters, a new pair of jeans, a pretty pair of earrings and another blanket for her bed. Then she'd found a craft store that carried art supplies and she'd bought herself drawing pencils, watercolors and paper. Amy had always taken shopping for granted. There had always been a checkbook with a bottomless balance or a stack of credit cards that Daddy would pay off every month. She had underwear in her dresser at home worth more than what she now made in a week.

But in all her life, she'd never felt so alive, so honest, as she did living on Brendan's boat. It was a perfectly simple life, with few responsibilities and many satisfactions. She was actually good at what she did. Brendan respected her intelligence. She felt an incredible sense of satisfaction when they completed a day of work.

At home, her master's degree in English literature had been frowned upon as a waste of time. Though her parents had supported her desire to go to college, they thought a post-graduate education was simply postponing the most important goal in her life—marriage to the right man and then three or four well-behaved children.

When she'd brought Craig home for the first time, her mother and father had been thrilled. He was from a fine New England family, and though he had rather radical ideas about his career path, they looked upon him as the first and best hope for their only child's future happiness. But her happiness had slowly dissolved in the face of her father's influence.

Brendan Quinn could never be influenced like that, Amy mused. He was his own man, a man who had worked his way up from a hardscrabble childhood to a career that was about to get him a slot on the *New York Times* bestseller list. Amy sighed softly. "Brendan Quinn." Just the sound of his name on her lips made her feel safe and warm.

Though she shouldn't think about things like imaginary meetings between her father and her lover, she'd grown so used to Brendan riding to her rescue, she just assumed he'd be there when she finally had to face her parents. And there would come a time when she'd have to face them. She just needed to wait a little longer, until the embarrassment of her canceled wedding wore off, until the inconvenience of having to hire private detectives to find her was forgotten. Until Craig understood that she had absolutely no intention of marrying him.

Amy groaned softly and pulled a pillow over her eyes. But she yanked it away when she heard voices coming from outside.

"Ahoy, Brendan Quinn!" a woman's voice called. "Permission to come aboard."

Amy scrambled to her knees and peered out the porthole above his berth, but it had frosted over in the night and she couldn't see a thing. With a soft curse, she jumped out of bed, wrapped herself in her new comforter and hurried through the main cabin to unlock the hatch. She stepped out into the cold. "Who is it?" she shouted.

A willowy blonde hopped up on deck followed by a pretty brunette. They looked at each other and then at Amy. "We were looking for Brendan," the blonde said.

Amy felt a flood of mortification as she stared at the two incredibly beautiful women. They were dressed for the cold in trendy jackets, jeans and boots, the kind of clothes she used to wear when she had more money. "He's not here," Amy said softly. "He had to go to New York. But I'd be happy to let him know that you stopped by."

"Are you Amy?" the brunette asked.

Amy blinked in surprise. "Yes."

"I told you Conor was lying," the brunette said with

a cluck of her tongue. She hurried across the deck and held out her hand. "I'm Meggie Flanagan. And this is Olivia Farrell—I mean, Olivia Quinn."

"Quinn?"

"I'm married to Conor, Brendan's older brother," the blonde explained. "You met him the other day. And Meggie is engaged to Dylan, another brother. You must be Brendan's new assistant." She held out a perfectly manicured hand.

Amy poked her own hand out from beneath the blanket, embarrassed by her chipped nail polish and her closely bitten nails. "I am," she said. "I'm Amy Aldrich."

Olivia paused as she shook her hand. "You aren't related to Mrs. Adele Aldrich, are you?"

Amy's heart stopped at the sound of her grandmother's name. She hadn't seen or talked to her grandmother since she'd run away. Over the past six months, she was the one person Amy had been tempted to call. Now the mere mention of her name made that need more acute. "I'm afraid we're not related," she said. "Why?"

"Adele is a client of mine," Olivia said. "I'm an antiques dealer and I help her find pieces for her house on Beacon Hill."

Amy ached to draw Olivia inside, to ask her about her grandmother's health and whether she'd visited with her recently. She wanted to know how her two cats were and whether she was planning a vacation for the winter months. "Would you like to come in?" she asked.

"Actually, we were here to talk Brendan into taking us out to lunch. But we'd love it if you joined us."

Amy glanced down at the blanket she was wearing, then ran her fingers through her tangled hair. "I'm really not ready to—"

"Oh, we'll wait," Meggie said cheerfully. "We're not in any hurry."

Amy wasn't sure why they'd want her to come to lunch with them. They didn't even know her. As far as they were concerned, she was just Brendan's assistant. "Come in out of the cold, then," she said. They both followed her into the cabin. She hurried over to the table in the galley and began to stack the mess of papers she'd left there. "Please, sit down. Can I make you a cup of coffee?"

Olivia shook her head and slid into a spot. "No, we're fine." She reached across the table, then pulled a thick piece of illustration paper from beneath a coffee mug and studied it carefully.

Amy groaned inwardly and reached out for the paper. "Oh, don't look at that. I was just...doodling."

Olivia glanced at the illustration, then back up at Amy. "You did this?"

She nodded. "I wanted to give Brendan something for Christmas and since I don't have a lot of cash, I thought I'd make him something. I found this book of stories that he had written out about his ancestors and I decided to—"

"The Mighty Quinns?" Meggie asked.

"Yes, the Mighty Quinns. I thought I'd illustrate them and put them into a book for him. That illustration is of a story about a giant named Fomor."

"That's a wonderful thing you're doing for Brendan," Olivia said. "You're very talented."

Amy felt a blush warm her cheeks. "It's nothing really. I took art lessons when I was young and I thought I'd pick it up again." She smoothed the front of the comforter then smiled. "Well, I'd better get ready. I can't believe I slept so late."

She rushed to her cabin and closed the door behind her, then began to frantically search for something to wear. They were both dressed so nicely and everything she owned looked shabby in comparison. She thought of her closets at home, filled with designer clothes, then sat down on the edge of the bed. "Look at you," she murmured. "All you've worked for brushed aside for two women in pretty clothes. The clothes don't define you. You define the clothes."

With a smile, Amy grabbed a pair of jeans and a pretty blue sweater and pulled them on. After running a brush through her hair, she decided against makeup, settling for a simple pair of earrings and a scarf to embellish her plain ponytail. When she emerged from her cabin, she felt confident again, certain she could handle any questions the two women had.

"There," she said. "So, have you been up here to see Brendan before?"

Olivia and Meggie looked at each other, then smiled apologetically. "We really didn't come up here to see Brendan," Meggie admitted. "We didn't even come to look for antiques. We came to see you."

"Me?" Amy nervously smoothed her palms over the front of her sweater, her confidence waning again. "Why?"

"Because you're Brendan's new girlfriend," Olivia explained. "And we wanted to check you out. It's impossible to get the straight story from Conor or Dylan. They just won't talk. And after we found out how you two met, well, we had to see if it was true."

"If what was true?"

"Did he carry you out of a bar?"

Amy nodded. "Yes."

They looked at each other again, then they both stood. "I think we should definitely have lunch," Olivia said. "A nice long lunch so we can really get to know each other. Wouldn't that be fun?"

Amy wasn't sure she wanted to have lunch with these ladies. They were acting very strangely, as if she were some new curiosity they'd discovered and now wanted to dissect. Despite that they seemed awfully nice. And she hadn't had any social contact with friends since she'd been fired from the Longliner. Though Brendan was great company, he didn't really like to talk about "girl" things. "That would be fun," Amy said.

They climbed out the hatch and Amy shut it behind her, then followed Olivia and Meggie off the boat. As they strolled down the dock, they chatted amiably, asking Amy all about herself, but never prying too deeply. Amy had never had a lot of close friends. Usually, people were interested in her only because her father was Avery Aldrich Sloane. But Olivia and Meggie had no idea who she was. As far as they were concerned, she was just a young woman who happened to work for Brendan Quinn.

Amy smiled to herself. It would be nice to have some

new friends. As they walked toward the wharf, she wondered if she and Olivia and Meggie might share something more than friendship. They were part of Brendan's family, like sisters to him. If she and Brendan had a future together, then they would be like sisters to her.

She brushed aside the thought, determined not to plan her life any more than a day in advance. If she continued to think about Brendan Quinn in those terms, she'd be setting herself up for heartache. But no matter how much she tried to convince herself to the contrary, Amy knew she loved him.

She just wasn't sure what to do with feelings she was unprepared to acknowledge, yet helpless to deny.

BRENDAN GLANCED at his watch for the third time in the last five minutes. The cab turned toward the waterfront from the train station and he knew he was only a few minutes away from home—and Amy. A light snow had been falling all the way from Boston, dusting everything with a layer of white that sparkled beneath the streetlights. He'd never gotten into the holiday spirit in the past, but for some reason, this holiday was different.

He told himself it was because of family plans with his brothers and Olivia and Meggie. But Brendan suspected that it had more to do with Amy. He wouldn't be alone on Christmas. She'd be there. He'd take her along to Boston on Christmas Eve and introduce her to the whole family. They'd drive back after midnight mass and then have a quiet Christmas of their own.

Brendan raked his hand through his hair as he stared

out the windows. He shouldn't be thinking like this, as if he and Amy shared more than just a temporary relationship. She was engaged to another man and he had a life that included months on the road. Neither one of them were free to make any commitments. But that didn't stop him from wanting to change those facts.

The cabbie pulled up near the pier where *The Mighty Quinn* was tied up. Brendan leaned over, paid the cabbie then grabbed his overnight bag and hopped out.

He saw the lights all the way down at the end of the dock. Brendan turned back to make sure he was on the right pier, then slowly walked toward his boat. He'd barely set a foot on board, when Amy appeared in the hatchway, her smile warm and welcoming.

"Do you like it?" she asked as she jumped out on the deck.

Brendan stared up at the lights, outlining every angle of the boat. She'd even strung lights up the radar mast and draped them out at angles until it looked like a Christmas tree. "It's very...twinkly," he said. "Where did you get all these lights?"

Her expression fell, her shoulders slumping. "You don't like it."

Brendan had to admit, it was a bit garish, especially for something as manly as a swordfishing boat. But it was also very festive. "I like it," Brendan said. "I don't think *The Mighty Quinn* has ever looked...prettier."

With a tiny cry of delight, Amy launched herself into his arms and gave him a fierce hug. But Brendan didn't want it to stop there. He wove his fingers through the hair at her nape and tipped her face up to his. Then he kissed her, slowly and gently, exactly the way he'd thought about kissing her on the long trip back from the city. And the way he'd thought about kissing her as he lay in his hotel room last night.

She tasted so good he wasn't willing to let her go, even though they were both standing out in the cold and damp. But Amy would have no more. She pulled away, then stared up into his eyes. "I have another surprise inside." She grabbed his hand and drew him toward the hatch.

The Christmas tree was tucked in a corner of the main cabin. The smell of fresh pine filled the air bringing back a long-ago memory—a tall tree in the front parlor of their house on Kilgore Street...his mother reaching up to hang tinsel...piles of presents beneath the tree. Brendan slowly walked over to the tree and ran his fingers along a row of needles.

"Is it all right?" Amy asked.

"It's perfect," he murmured.

She clapped her hands and smiled. "Wait. This is the best part." She hurried over to the bulkhead, then flipped the switch for the main cabin lighting. The cabin went dark except for the lights twinkling on the tree. Amy came up behind him and wrapped her arms around his waist. "I like it when the lights are off," she murmured. "That was always the best part. Sitting in the dark with just the Christmas tree lit."

He turned in her arms and gazed down at her pretty face illuminated only by the lights from the tree. She'd had a childhood, a childhood she remembered fondly, yet here she was with him, far away from those she knew. Brendan bent down and dropped a kiss on her lips, then smoothed his palm over her cheek.

How had this happened, he wondered. When he'd brought her onboard he'd resolved that any attraction between them would be set aside. He'd been determined to stick to that plan. Yet here he was, eager to lose himself in her kisses, desperate to touch her, thoroughly and completely in love with Amy Aldrich.

"Who are you?" he murmured, dropping a line of kisses along the soft skin beneath her ear.

"I'm anyone you want me to be," she replied.

She reached up and pushed her palms beneath his jacket brushing it off his shoulders. Brendan took his hands off of her just long enough for the jacket to fall to the floor. Then she began on his tie, working at the knot with her fingers. Though he wanted to tear it off himself, he schooled his impatience and enjoyed watching her slowly undress him.

His shirt followed his tie and his belt followed his shirt. As she pressed her lips to his chest, Brendan furrowed his fingers through her hair and tipped her head back. He'd never wanted a woman more than he wanted Amy. She was sweet and passionate and her touch drove him wild with need. But though he knew her intimately, from the tiny mole just above her left breast to the scar on her right knee, all he really knew of her was what they'd shared.

To him, Amy had no past. She'd blown into his life like a storm and he had every reason to believe she'd blow right back out. But he was going to do his best to hold on to her while he could.

She traced a lazy line of kisses to his belly, sucking

and nipping, sending a shiver of sensation through his body. Then she worked open the front of his trousers, slowly pulling the zipper down and sliding her hands beneath the fabric until she'd pushed it, and his boxers, away from his hips.

Brendan knew what was coming and he even anticipated how it would feel to have her mouth on him. But when it happened, when she took him with her lips and her tongue, a shock so strong and electric raced through him that he wasn't sure he'd be able to stand, much less breathe. He braced his arms on the edge of the galley counter, gripping it with white-knuckled hands.

Slowly, she seduced him, bringing him nearer and nearer to the edge, then slowly drawing him back to safety. Time and again, he thought he'd explode, but Amy seemed to sense his desire and controlled him until he was almost mad with need. Then, she brought him too close and he felt as if he couldn't wait any longer. Gently, but firmly, he drew her up to her feet, capturing her sweet mouth and kissing her deeply. "I want you," he murmured against her damp lips.

"You already have me," she said.

Brendan bunched her sweater in his fists, then yanked it over her head, breaking their kiss for only a moment. He tossed the sweater aside, then reached for her jeans, unbuttoning them and skimming them down over her hips in one smooth but impatient motion. Amy kicked them aside, then reached up and wrapped her arms around his neck, drawing him toward one of the sofa berths that flanked the main cabin.

He kicked off the rest of his clothes, leaving them on the floor of the galley. Her hands smoothed over his body, exploring every inch of skin until he felt as if his nerves were on fire. Brendan couldn't help but wonder at the power of their desire. Though they'd made love many times over the past few days, it never seemed to fade. Their need only grew stronger, more desperate.

It wasn't so much the physical release that he craved anymore. It was the intimate connection, the way he could almost touch her soul when he was inside her. Everything in life became so simple when he was lying with Amy, reduced to basic needs. He'd always thought love was supposed to be complicated, yet with Amy, it was easy. As easy as breathing.

As he looked down at her, stretched out on the sofa berth, a lazy smile curling her lips, Brendan fought the urge to tell her how he felt. He wanted to say the words. *I love you.* Even they were simple. But instinct told him to wait. Combined with the intensity of their desire, such a proclamation might frighten her off. And the last thing he wanted was to send her running before she realized her own feelings for him.

He had no doubt that he could make her fall in love with him. He could make her forget her past and build a future with him. But before he'd ever do that, Brendan had to be sure that she needed him as much as he needed her. He bent closer and brushed a kiss across her lips and she moaned impatiently.

Brendan did away with the tiny scraps of lace and satin that she called underwear. But as he caressed her curves, he wanted to please her in the same way she'd pleased him. He stared down at her beautiful body, the soft flesh illuminated by the twinkling lights of her Christmas tree. His lips found her breast, drawing her nipple into his mouth until it hardened into a nub.

Then, as she had teased him, he moved down to her stomach, to her hip and finally to the damp juncture between her thighs. Gently, he made love to her in a new way, a way that brought a deeper intimacy to their passion. Amy arched against him, her hands raking through his hair, drawing him nearer then pushing him away, calling his name in whispered pleas and asking him for her release.

When he knew she was there, Brendan moved above her and then inside her, not bothering with protection, aching to feel every sensation intensely and without barriers. He knew he shouldn't, but he couldn't help himself. Amy was his, for now and forever. The thought pulsed through his mind as he slowly withdrew, then plunged again into her damp heat. She was his...she was his.

They were both so close that their lovemaking didn't last long. Amy came first, convulsing around him, crying out as she reached her peak, her voice pushing him to his own climax. The explosion wracked his body, every muscle tensed for an exquisite moment and then released with a rush of warmth.

When he was completely spent, he lay down beside her and threw his leg over her hips. They didn't say a word, instead communicating with fleeting kisses and gentle caresses. Brendan hadn't realized until this moment what happiness was, what true contentment meant. When his brothers had found it, he thought them fools, swept away by emotions that would soon fade.

But now he was caught in the same swirl of emotion, determined to make a future for himself with the woman who had brought him here. Brendan nuzzled Amy's neck and sighed softly. He'd make it happen, if it took every ounce of his determination. Amy was his—and nothing could make him give her up.

"You should really get your Christmas shopping done early," Amy scolded. She reached up and straightened an ornament on the Christmas tree, then stood back and looked at it. "Christmas is two weeks away and you're going to want time to choose something perfect for your family members."

"I don't have any Christmas shopping to do," Brendan said as he spread the newspaper on the galley table. "Remember, I'm a Scrooge."

"You *were* a Scrooge," she said, giving him a coy smile. "But I'm reforming you. Marcie and Olivia are probably going to buy you a gift. You're going to have to find something for them."

"How do you know that? You're not my best friends with them after just—"

"No," Amy replied. "But I know what kind of people they are. They're the kind of family who would be thoughtful enough to buy a gift for their bah-humbug new father-in-law. So if you don't want to buy Christmas gifts, just give gifts to those who do. And give them in return. So you're going to go out and shop," she said.

"You'll know what they like. It's part of your job as my assistant."

"I barely know them."

"But you're a woman," he said. "You know them better than I do."

Amy crossed the cabin and grabbed his hand. "Come on. We've worked hard enough today. We'll walk into town and see what we can find. Jewelry is always a nice gift. Or a pretty sweater. If we don't find anything today, then I'll do your shopping for you."

Brendan pulled her down onto his lap, and nuzzled her neck. In the past, he couldn't have thought of anything he'd dread more than shopping with a woman. But Amy made it sound fun. "We can shop later. Let's find something better to do."

Amy wriggled out of his arms. "If we're going to stay on the boat, then we're going to work. We're almost finished with your book. It might be nice to get it done early. Then you can enjoy the holidays."

Brendan stared down at the newspaper, the text blurring in front of his eyes. She was right. The book was nearly done and once it was, there was nothing keeping her with him. He wasn't ready to face that fact yet, wasn't even close to letting her go. "I've been thinking. Maybe we should take another pass at the book. Just to make sure it's really the best it can be."

Amy sent him a grateful smile. "I know what you're doing," she said.

"What's that?"

"Dragging your feet. Trying to delay so that you can give me more time to find a new job. I'll be all right," she said. "I'll find something else. I've been thinking a lot about your offer to talk to your publisher."

"New York?"

She shrugged. "Why not?" Amy grabbed his jacket from the sofa berth and handed it to him. "We'll talk about that later," she said. "Let's go. We'll do some shopping and afterward, you can take me out to lunch."

Brendan grabbed his jacket, then helped her slip into hers. As they stepped out on deck, the sun warmed their faces and a breeze, almost balmy, buffeted the water of the harbor. It was a perfect day, snow melting on the sidewalks and water dripping off the eaves of the buildings into puddles at their feet. They walked into town and headed toward some of the small gift shops that catered to the summer tourists.

Amy paused at the window of one of the shops, dragging him to a stop. "This is nice," she said, pointing to a display of jewelry.

"Earrings?"

"All of it. It's by a local artist and the jewelry is made of sea glass. I stopped in the other day and looked at it. It's really pretty. But it's a little expensive."

"What's sea glass?" Brendan asked.

"It's glass from the sea. Bits and pieces that wash up on the beach, some of it very old. And the waves and the sand burnish it until it almost looks like a jewel. I know Meggie and Olivia would love something like this."

"How do you know?"

Amy laughed. "Because *I* would love something like this," she said.

Brendan nodded. "All right. Wait here."

She grabbed his hand. "But I'll come in and help you pick something out."

"No, I can do that on my own. Wait here."

Brendan stepped inside the shop and walked over to the display case on the far wall, determined to get this shopping business over as quickly as possible. The saleslady smiled and hurried over to help him, obviously glad to have a customer at this time of year. "I'd like to buy some of your sea glass jewelry," he said.

She removed a velvet-covered board from the case and set it on top of the counter. "This is handcrafted by a local artist," she said. "And all of the—"

"I'll take two pairs of earrings," he interrupted.

"Which ones?"

Brendan frowned, then shrugged. "Any ones. Pretty ones. You pick them out. And wrap them." The saleslady did as she was asked and as Brendan waited impatiently, his gaze wandered to the necklaces. He stopped when he saw a beautiful silver pendant with a large piece of blue glass in it. When the saleslady returned with his purchases, he pointed at the spot in the case. "Can I look at that necklace? The one with the blue stone?"

She reached inside the case and pulled it out to hand to him. "That's a lovely piece. You know the blue glass is very rare."

Brendan glanced over his shoulder. Amy was standing at the window, her back to them. "Do you think she would like it?" Brendan asked.

The saleslady looked at the window, then back at

Brendan. "I think a beautiful gift from a handsome man would make any woman very happy."

He held the necklace up. The glass was the exact color of Amy's eyes. He'd never bought a gift for a woman before. The notion had always seemed so serious and he'd never wanted to create the wrong impression—that he cared. He couldn't count the number of women who had passed through his life, hanging around for a few weeks then moving on. And never once, had he considered buying them a necklace.

"I'll take it," he said. "But you don't need to wrap it."

The saleslady put the necklace in a tiny box, then Brendan slipped it in his pocket and handed her a credit card. When he was finished, he turned to the door, thanking her for her help. Amy was waiting outside. She hurried up to him and slipped her arm though his.

"Show me what you bought," she said.

"Why?"

"So I can make sure it's all right."

Brendan frowned. "What if it isn't all right?"

"Then we'll take it back and get something else."

"I agreed to go shopping," he said. "And I assumed that meant buying, not returning."

"Just show me what you bought," she insisted.

"Well, I bought two pairs of earrings. And then I bought this." Brendan reached in his jacket pocket and pulled out the small box, then handed it to her. Amy removed the lid, then plucked out the delicate silver chain. She held the necklace up and sighed. "It's beautiful."

"It's for you," he said.

Amy blinked, her gaze darting between him and the necklace. "For me?"

"It's a present. I probably should have waited until Christmas to give it to you, but I'm not very good at keeping secrets. So I want you to have it now."

"But—but why?"

"Because I do," Brendan said. He took the necklace from her fingers, then clumsily worked open the clasp. "Turn around."

She did as she was told and he slipped the necklace around her neck and fastened it. Slowly, she turned back to him, a winsome smile touching her lips. "Thank you," she said, staring down at the pendant.

"It's blue," Brendan commented awkwardly. "Just like your eyes. Do you like it?"

She glanced up at him and he saw tears shimmering in those eyes. At first, he was certain that he'd done something wrong, but then she threw her arms around her neck and gave him a fierce hug. "I couldn't love anything more," she murmured.

As they stood in front of the shop, wrapped in each others arms, Brendan could only wish that her words were meant for him and not for the necklace. He hugged her tight. "Neither could I," he murmured. "Neither could I."

7

BRENDAN SAT AT the Sandpiper Cafe near Gloucester's waterfront, staring out the window at the winter fog that had settled over the village. Conor had called early that morning, asking to meet him for breakfast, but he had refused Brendan's offer to drive into the city. Instead, Conor wanted to meet him in Gloucester. Brendan suspected that his brother had found something disturbing about Amy and wanted to speak to him closer to home.

Brendan could only assume it was bad news. He'd prepared himself on the walk over, convinced that Amy had lied and she was married. Or that she had done something against the law. Or that she really was some kind of con artist as Conor had first suspected. But as he waited for Conor to arrive, he'd convinced himself that it made no difference, that nothing, no matter how bad, could undermine his feelings for her.

Was he a fool? Or was he so determined to make Amy part of his life that he was blind to the obvious? Hell, they'd known each other ten days and he was already so certain of her innocence that he was ready to risk it all for a chance at a future. Had anyone told him he'd fall so fast and so hard, he would have laughed in their face. But it seemed when a Quinn brother found a woman to love, the courtship progressed at lightning speed.

The waitress stopped by the table and freshened his coffee, then offered him a menu. Brendan poured sugar and cream into his cup and slowly stirred as he watched the door. A few seconds later, Conor strode in, wearing a tailored suit and a tie. Since he'd been promoted to homicide, he'd been dressing a lot better on the job, though Brendan guessed that Olivia had more to do with the change in his fashion sense than his superiors. Hell, he nearly looked respectable.

Conor surveyed the patrons sitting along the counter, then caught sight of Brendan in a booth and walked over to his table. As he sat down, he nodded to the waitress for coffee.

"What did you find out?" Brendan asked, leaning forward and trying to read his brother's expression.

"What?" Conor chuckled. "No happy greeting? No chitchat about Olivia?"

Brendan cursed softly. "Hi, how are you, you're looking well, how's Olivia. There, feel better? Now, what did you find out?"

The waitress returned with coffee and Brendan tapped his foot impatiently, waiting for her to leave. When she did, Conor reached inside his breast pocket, pulled out a thick envelope and tossed it across the table at Brendan. He stared down at it, suddenly unsure that he wanted to open what looked suspiciously like a Pandora's box. Maybe it would be best to continue on without knowing the truth. He'd gotten this far, why not just leave the past in the past?

"Are you afraid?" Conor asked. "Because if you are, I'll open it for you."

"I'm not afraid," Brendan shot back. "It's just that—"

"You're in love with her and you'd kinda like to know who the hell she is," Conor completed. "Well, I'll tell you. Are you ready for this? She's an heiress."

Brendan wasn't quite sure he'd heard his brother right. He was expecting convicted felon...or fugitive from justice...or petty criminal. "What do you mean?"

"Just what I said. Her real name is Amelia Aldrich Sloane. Her father is Avery Aldrich Sloane of Aldrich Industries. Her grandmother is Adele Aldrich of the Aldrich wing at Boston General and the Aldrich Pavilion at Symphony Hall and the Aldrich Gallery at the Museum of Fine Art."

"Amy is *that* Aldrich?"

"She's from a wealthy Boston family and she'll inherit a few million from a trust fund in May. And when Daddy Sloane dies, she'll inherit the whole enchilada. She'll be one of the richest women in Boston."

Brendan raked his hands through his hair. "Why the hell is she on the run?" A curse slipped from his lips and anger bubbled inside of him. "All this time I've been worrying about her past, wondering what she's hiding, fearing that the cops were going to come knocking at the door. And she's hiding the fact that she's *rich?*"

"Maybe she doesn't want the money?" Conor replied with a shrug.

"Who the hell wouldn't want that kind of money?" Brendan asked. He lowered his voice when he noticed other patrons turning to stare. "What about the fiancé?"

"Craig Atkinson Talbot." Conor chuckled as he opened the envelope. "Why do rich people always have three names?" He handed Brendan a page from a report. "Another prominent Boston family. The Beacon Hill Talbots. Their money comes from banking, though not nearly in the quantity of the Aldrich Sloane fortune. Amy disappeared a week before they were scheduled to be married. At first, her parents thought she was kidnapped and the police were on the case for awhile until they figured out she ran away of her own accord. That's when Daddy Sloane sent out his hired guns to find her."

"She's an adult. She can do what she wants," Brendan said. "He can't make her come back."

"Bren, I don't think you or I really understand that kind of family. We're from Southie and we had nobody telling us what we could and couldn't do. We had nowhere to go but up. But money like that is an obligation. You don't just walk away. She's the only child of Mr. Moneybags himself. I would guess there's plenty of pressure not to marry the local video store clerk."

Brendan stared at the picture of Amy and her fiancé. "And you just don't marry the son of an Irish swordfisherman either. Or a writer who never knows where his next paycheck is coming from."

"Don't start that," Conor warned. "I worried about the same thing with Olivia, but if you love someone, it doesn't make a difference."

"Olivia isn't an heiress with a father who could buy and sell us both with his pocket change."

"And I'm not a famous writer," Conor said. "You're not just some working-class bum. You've got a career. People know you. That has to count for something."

Brendan stared out the window, the fog so thick now that the streetlights had come on. "Obviously, Amy doesn't think it's enough or she would have told me the truth."

"You don't know her reasons, so don't jump to conclusions."

Brendan had been prepared for bad news, but he wasn't sure what kind of news this was. He hadn't fallen in love with Amy Aldrich, former cocktail waitress and aspiring editor. He'd fallen in love with the heir to a Boston dynasty. Him, Brendan Quinn, working-class Irish boy straight from the old country. "You're pretty quick to defend her now," Brendan said. "You were telling me to get rid of her just a week ago."

"She's not a criminal. And she's never even come close to breaking the law, unless you count the tax ramifications of you paying her in cash." Conor leaned back in the booth. "What are you going to do about this? Are you going to tell her you know?"

Brendan shrugged. "I haven't figured that out yet." He reached for his coffee and took a long sip then looked at his brother. "I have to go."

"I know," Conor said. "Why don't you come down to the pub tonight? Bring Amy along. Olivia would love to see her again and I'm sure Maggie would, too. They have high hopes for this girl."

"Maybe," Brendan said, his answer meant only to pacify his brother. He slid out of the booth, tossed a few dollars on the table for their coffees and gave Conor a pat on the shoulder. "Thanks, Con. I appreciate what you did."

"I'm glad it turned out all right," he said.

Brendan smiled ruefully. "That has yet to be seen." He turned, walked to the door and stepped out on the street. The day was warm for December, the temperature causing the thick fog that rolled over the harbor. He strolled along the main street, his mind drifting back to the first night he'd seen her.

His first impression of Amy had been correct. She didn't belong at the Longliner, slinging drinks and fending off wandering hands. She came from a better life, a life that shanty Irish like the Quinns would never know. Suddenly, all his childhood insecurities came back. And along with them came the defensive streak that he and his brothers employed when they felt inferior. Anger surged up inside of him at his childhood circumstances.

Though he didn't know Avery Aldrich Sloane, he knew enough about men like him to predict how he'd react. His little girl wasn't meant to waste her life on a man like Brendan Quinn. He had better prospects in mind for her. Brendan cursed softly. Even his single-minded determination paled in comparison to a few million dollars.

When he reached the waterfront, he stood at the end of the dock for a long time. Would he look at her differently now that he knew her real name? "Amelia Aldrich Sloane," he murmured. He couldn't seem to reconcile the name, the heiress, with the Amy he knew.

He started down the dock and as he came nearer to

The Mighty Quinn, he noticed Amy standing on top of the pilothouse, high above the deck. "What the hell are you doing up there?" he shouted.

She turned and looked down at him, then waved. "Look!" she cried. "I found this at the hardware store." She stepped aside and he saw a big plastic Santa standing on top of the pilothouse, lit up like a beacon in the fog. "Isn't it wonderful? At night, you're going to be able to see it all over the waterfront."

"And that's a good thing?" Brendan asked.

"You don't like it?" she asked.

"Just come down," he said impatiently. He held his breath as she crawled down the ladder to the deck. When she jumped down beside him, her cheeks were rosy with the cold and her hair curly from the damp. She threw her arms around his neck and gave him an enthusiastic kiss, but Brendan felt himself draw away. She was different to him now that he knew the truth. And he wasn't sure whether he ought to be angry or hurt.

Why had she kept something so important from him? So she had money. Did she really try to take advantage? He made enough on the boat that he didn't want for anything. Or maybe it was something else. Maybe rich girls like Amy Aldrich just enjoyed the thrill of slumming, sleeping with someone well below their social class, then walking away without a second thought.

"I just needed a focal point," she explained, "and there up at the place I couldn't resist. I saw it on my way back from the hardware store. It was only five dollars."

"Imagine that," he said, a sarcastic edge to his voice. "Well, if the harbor lights break down, we can guide boats in with our illuminated Santa." He started toward the hatch.

"Maybe I should have gone with something more religious," she said, following after him. "They had a manger scene but I didn't think it would fit. Besides, Santa is a good antidote to your humbug attitude. How can you look at that face and not smile?"

He stared down at her pretty heart-shaped face, his anger fading. Though he ought to be wary, all he felt was relief at Conor's news. She wasn't married, she wasn't a criminal. There might be a chance for a future with her. "I can't," he murmured. For a few moments, he forgot everything that he'd learned in the restaurant. He just couldn't see her living in a mansion with servants catering to her every whim. He couldn't imagine her in fancy clothes and expensive jewelry, driving a luxury sports car. The only Amy he knew was the Amy who had shared his bed.

Brendan pulled her into his embrace and wrapped his arms around her. "You're cold," he said, drawing a ragged breath. Then he pressed a kiss to her temple.

For a long moment, he didn't want to let her go, afraid that she would somehow change before his eyes and become a stranger to him. He'd been so determined to confront her, but now that she was near, nothing seemed to matter but the feel of her body in his arms. Brendan knew he was risking his heart, by loving a woman who might never be able to love him in return. But even after all the lies, he had to believe what he saw in her face, what he had heard in her voice

...they made love. Amy Aldrich needed him, as much as he needed her.

"Come on," Brendan said. "Let's go inside. We've got a lot of work to do."

AMY WATCHED Brendan from the warmth of his bed as he moved about his cabin, picking up clothes from the floor and folding them neatly. He'd just crawled out of bed and he hadn't bothered to put on anything, yet he was completely at ease with his nakedness.

He had an incredible body, hard and lean and muscular, with broad shoulders and narrow hips. Amy had always considered physical attributes less important in a relationship than an emotional connection. But there was something about touching a man so perfect, so utterly male, that could set her heart racing and her pulse pounding. She loved his mind and his heart and his soul, but his body drove her wild in the bedroom.

"You're beautiful," Amy said.

Brendan glanced over his shoulder. "What?"

"You're beautiful," she repeated. "I never thought a man could be beautiful. I mean, they are in a classical sense. Like Michelangelo's David. But when you stand in the right light, you look so...perfect. I could stare at you all day and not get enough."

"I don't mind when you look," he said. "But I like it much better when you touch."

And they'd done plenty of that the night before. His mind drifted back, remembering the way he'd touched her with such a single-minded determination. His lovemaking was different from previous nights, more purposeful, as if he were trying to prove and memorize every moment. He'd be gentle, then frantic, then demanding, taking every ounce of her passion until she was completely spent. It was as if he were making love to her for the last time.

Lately, Amy had begun to wonder if there would be a last time. They hadn't talked about her leaving for the past few days. The book was essentially done but they'd both created a pretense that it wasn't, finding little make-work jobs to keep them busy during the day, then tumbling into bed together at night to enjoy each other's body.

But how long could this go on? Sooner or later, Brendan would have to put the book in the mail and then her work would be over. In truth, Amy wasn't even sure he had another project lined up. When she'd asked him, he'd been short and dismissive, so she'd taken that as a "no."

"I'm going to take a shower," Brendan said. "Do you want to come with me?"

Amy laughed, then snuggled down beneath the covers. "There's barely enough room in that shower for one person. I don't think we'd fit."

"We could try," he said, as if this were one more excuse he was determined to find.

"Why don't you take a shower and I'll make us some lunch."

He crawled onto the bed and gave her a long and lingering kiss. "Sounds like a good idea." He pushed up and grabbed a fresh towel from the shelf near the bed and walked to the head. Amy pulled one of his old shirts around her and padded out into the main

She crossed over to the galley table and stared down at the work scattered there. It hadn't even been two weeks since she'd first set foot on *The Mighty Quinn*, yet it seemed like a lifetime ago. For twenty-five years her days and months and years had passed at a measured pace, but now every moment seemed to fly by, hurling her toward the time when she and Brendan would be forced to walk away from each other.

"Ask me to stay," she murmured, "and I will."

She was startled out of her thoughts by the sound of Brendan's cell phone ringing. She reached for the phone on the table and flipped it open. "Brendan Quinn's phone," she said.

"Is Brendan there?" a male voice asked.

Amy glanced over her shoulder at the door to the head, but she could hear the water running inside. "I'm afraid he's not available right now," Amy said. "I'm his assistant. Can I take a message?"

"Tell him Rob Sargeant called. I'm his agent. The trip to Turkey has been moved up. He's supposed to be there on the twenty-third, two weeks earlier than we originally discussed. The dig will last for four months, so he should be back before that wedding in June."

"Four months?" Amy asked. "In Turkey?"

"He needs to get his visa in order," the agent continued, "and I've got an airline ticket here at the office that I'll send overnight. I suppose I can coordinate most of these things with you?"

"Of—of course," Amy said, struggling to make her voice work. "I am his assistant."

"Fine," Rob said. "We'll speak in the next few days

...ding other arrangements that need to be made. ... Brendan to call me later today."

"Goodbye," Amy murmured. She turned off the phone and set it in front of her. With a soft sigh, she ...ssed her palm to her heart and tried to absorb the ...ws. Of course he wasn't going to ask her to stay be-cause he was leaving! Brendan was leaving the country ...d he'd never even mentioned it to her.

If he knew he was going to walk away, then why did ... act as if he cared? Why did he allow things to be-...me so serious? Amy closed her eyes and cursed her-..., remembering the first time they had made love. It ...been simply sex then and she'd assured him that it ...nt nothing to her. "This was what you wanted," ... murmured. "This was exactly what you asked for. ...ings, no attachments."

...t she couldn't help feeling betrayed, as if he'd ...d her into caring about him. No wonder he was so ...us to find her a new job. It would be the easiest ...y to avoid a bad case of guilt. He'd known all along ...t their affair would be short-lived. Yet she'd stu-...ly imagined it might be more. Tears pressed at the ...ers of her eyes and she sat down on the sofa berth ...d pulled her knees up under the baggy shirt.

Amy wasn't sure how long she sat there, staring at ...thing, her mind swirling with doubts and regret. But ...hen Brendan walked into the main cabin, rubbing his ...mp hair with a towel, another towel riding low on ...ips, she glanced up and forced a smile. She wasn't ... allow him to see how she really felt.

...lked over to the ... ...bbed a ... orange juice, then ... e her and took a drink from the carton. "I thought you were going to make lunch," he said.

"I was," she murmured. "But then I got distracted. Your agent just called."

Brendan took another sip of the juice. "What did he want?"

"He said your trip to Turkey is all set. But you have to leave on the twenty-third. Two days before Christmas." She swallowed hard, fighting back a surge of emotion. "You'll need some time to get ready and to pack. I told him that I'd help with all the arrangements...since that's my job...as your assistant." She bit her bottom lip, fighting back the tears. "Why didn't you tell me?"

Brendan cursed softly, then caught her chin with his thumb and turned her gaze to his. "I guess I should have," he murmured.

"No," Amy said, drawing a deep breath and trying to appear indifferent. "You had no reason to mention it. And I have no reason to care. I knew the job was short-term, so that's that. Turkey. Well, that sounds exciting."

He raked his hand through his damp hair. "I should have told you," he insisted. "It's just that I wasn't quite sure about the trip."

"Well, now you are," Amy said. She pasted a bright smile on her face. "And since you're leaving in a week, we have a lot of things to take care of. We'll have to get the book ready to send and you should spend some time with your family. And I'll need you to write that letter of recommendation and I'm going to have to go into the city and find a new place to live and —"

Brendan reached out and pressed a finger to her lips. "What about us?" he asked.

"Us?"

"We have to figure out what we're going to do about us, Amy."

She shifted uneasily. She had just assumed there wouldn't be an "us," that Brendan would leave and that would be the end of it. What was she supposed to do? Did he want her to wait for him? Given the choice, she would have stayed on *The Mighty Quinn* with Brendan until her feelings became clear. But now that wasn't an option.

"You could come with me," Brendan suggested. He reached out and took her hands in his. "It would be fun. We'd be together and we could do some traveling. There are so many things to see in Turkey."

"You want me to come as your assistant?" Amy asked.

"Why not? We work well together and I'm not sure I could write another book without you."

"And who would pay my salary?" she asked.

"I would. The same way I do now."

Amy pushed up off the sofa berth, then crossed her arms beneath her breasts. "And I would work for you? And I would be your lover? And we would go on as we have so far?"

"Yes," he said. "Unless you want something more. Do you want something more?" he asked, watching her closely, his gaze searching her face.

"I'd be dependent on you," she said.

"No." Brendan sighed in frustration. "We'd be partners. We'd be together. I need your help, Amy."

"But I'd be living your life. Your dreams." She turned away. How could he ask her to do this? She'd worked so hard for her independence and now she was ready to throw it all away for the passion she felt when she was in Brendan Quinn's arms. He hired her to do a job and she had done more than her share to help him, but now that was over.

Suddenly she felt pressured, as if everything between them might end the moment he stepped on a plane and flew out of her life. Was this what she really wanted, to trust her future to another man, to depend on someone else for her happiness? Or could she hold on to the life she'd created for herself and still be with Brendan?

Amy considered his proposition for a long moment. A few weeks ago, she would have jumped at the chance. What better adventure than to take off for Turkey and an archaeological dig? And getting out of the country would solve a few more problems. But now, her decision couldn't be taken so lightly. There was more involved, feelings that were becoming harder and harder to deny.

"I don't know," Amy murmured.

"What's to think about? You'd be getting paid, we'd be together."

"And what would you be paying me for?" Amy snapped. "My skills as an assistant or my presence in your bedroom?"

Her question seemed to take him by surprise. "Amy, you know that's not how I think of our...arrangement."

"That's a nice term for it. Arrangement. I guess I would have called it a relationship by now."

"You're the one who didn't want a relationship," he accused. "If you've changed your mind, then we've got a lot more to talk about than Turkey."

"No," she snapped. "I haven't changed my mind. It's just that you could have told me about your trip. I feel like you lied to me. I feel like I was just a convenient diversion before you took off for parts unknown."

Brendan laughed harshly as he stood up. "I lied to you? What about all the lies you've told me? That your family is living in California? That you went to junior college there?"

"What are you talking about?" Amy asked, a sudden wave of apprehension rushing through her.

"I know everything," Brendan said. "I know who you are. Amelia Aldrich Sloane, daughter of Avery Aldrich Sloane. Granddaughter of Adele Aldrich. Heiress to a huge fortune. You ran away from your life six months ago and you ended up here."

Amy couldn't believe what he was saying. He'd known about her? "Since when? How long have you known?"

"Awhile," Brendan murmured. "One of your father's private detectives approached me on the dock and gave me a photo of you and your fiancé. What's his name? Greg? Craig? I had Conor look into your background. He gave me most of the information a few days ago."

Amy stepped up to him, her body trembling with

anger, her fists clenched. "How dare you have me investigated!"

"Oh, this is choice," Brendan said, a sarcastic edge to his voice. "You're angry at me for having you investigated. I'm the one who gave you a place to live and a job. I was getting tired of waiting for you to tell me who the hell you were. For all I knew, I was harboring a criminal."

"Well, you must be so glad that you're harboring an heiress instead. Tell me, how long will it be before you claim the reward? There is a reward, isn't there? If there isn't I'll be very disappointed in my daddy. He does love to throw money at a problem in the hopes he can make it disappear."

"Your father is concerned about you," Brendan said.

"Don't you tell me about my father," she shot back.

"You should be glad that he cares. Hell, my father barely remembered he had children. He'd wander in every few months, leave some money and head back out again. We had nothing, we had *less* than nothing."

"You had each other," Amy said. "I had nobody. My parents ran my life and I was expected to do everything they asked. And when I set out on my own path—when I decided to marry Craig—they corrupted that. You think just because my family has money that life was somehow easier? Well it wasn't."

Brendan cursed. "Why are we yelling at each other?" he asked.

Amy stamped her foot. "Because I'm angry!"

"Well, I'm not," he said. "I don't care whether you're an heiress or a waitress. It doesn't make a difference to me."

"It will," she said.

"I won't let it." Brendan paused. "You haven't answered my question."

"I don't remember your question."

"You wanted to run away. That's why you ended up here," Brendan said. "So run away with me. Your father will never find you in Turkey."

Amy drew a shaky breath. She wanted to say yes. It all sounded so tempting, so exciting. She wanted to throw her future into his hands, to trust the love that she felt growing in her heart and hope that someday, he'd feel the same. She wanted to believe that if they loved each other, he'd still always value her independence as much as she did. But in the end, this wasn't her life, it was his.

"I can't," Amy said. "I just can't."

With that she turned on her heel and hurried toward her cabin. She slammed the door behind her and leaned back against it. Tears tumbled from her eyes and she brushed them away with a frustrated curse. She'd made the right decision. Though she might love him now, she'd only come to resent him later, when she realized that she was living his life. And he'd never mentioned anything about his own feelings. For all she knew, they'd get to Turkey and he'd decide he didn't need an assistant. Then where would she be?

She'd be without Brendan Quinn. She'd be without passion and desire and excitement in her life. So why not go with him? She'd wanted an adventure and this certainly would be one. And if things didn't work out, she'd come home—to whatever home she could make for herself. If she didn't have any expectations, then how could she be disappointed?

"How am I supposed to know?" she murmured.

A STRAINED SILENCE had settled over *The Mighty Quinn* as Amy and Brendan finished the final changes on his book. She'd slept in her own cabin last night and when he'd checked on her in the middle of the night, Brendan found her curled up into a tight little ball as if she needed to protect herself, even in sleep.

Suddenly, the Amy he knew, the spontaneous, clever, passionate Amy, was gone, replaced by a woman whose eyes flickered with apprehension and whose body stiffened every time he touched her. Brendan wasn't sure what to do. He'd tried to talk to her, but nothing he said seemed to crack the wall of indifference. She blamed him for something but he couldn't figure out what. Was she angry because he had found out the truth about her? Or because he asked her to come to Turkey with him?

Brendan stared down at the manuscript page that he'd been trying to read for the past hour. He'd been going over it again and again in his head, trying to decide on his next move. A few days ago, he might have asked her to marry him, but now he wasn't sure she even cared for him, much less loved him. And he wasn't sure he was ready to take on her family. He'd struggled long and hard to make something of himself, to believe he was good enough. But was he really good enough to marry Amy Aldrich Sloane?

Brendan suspected it was pride that was holding him back. From the start, he'd been the protector, the provider, the one to make Amy's life safe and secure. But in truth, she could buy anything she needed. Nothing he could provide would match what she could give herself.

Was he willing to become a kept man? Though he made a good living, it wasn't enough to keep her in the style to which she was accustomed. Hell, he lived on a damn boat. She probably had closets at home larger than *The Mighty Quinn*.

Brendan sighed. Amy had been right, though he'd been reluctant to admit it. The money *did* make a difference. Even now, he could see into their future. First, he'd let her pay for a new car. Then maybe a vacation here and there. And suddenly, it would be a huge house and another car and summers in the Mediterranean.

"I'm going to take the Christmas tree down."

Brendan looked up to find Amy standing near the forward companionway. "What?"

"The Christmas tree," she repeated. "Since you're not going to be here for Christmas, it will have to come down sometime. And the lights outside. I thought I could do that for you today."

"No," Brendan said.

"But, you can't leave it until the last—"

"Damn it, Amy, no!" He ran his fingers through his hair and closed his eyes, trying to school his temper. "Just leave it. You don't have to do that."

"I'm just trying to help," she shot back.

For a brief moment, he saw the old Amy, the girl filled with fire and passion, the stubborn hellcat he'd hauled out of the Longliner. "I want to leave the decorations up," he said. "I like them. And I've still got a week before they have to come down."

She crossed the cabin and held out a piece of paper to him. "I've made a list of things you'll need to do. I expect that you have someone who watches the boat while you're gone. You'll have to go to the post office and put a hold on your box. And you should probably make plans to see your family before you leave. And—"

"Stop," Brendan said. "I know how to handle this. I've left town before for a lot longer than four months. I know what needs to be done."

"I was just trying to—"

"Help," he finished. "Yes. I appreciate that."

She stared down at him, her gaze wary. "Did you write that letter of recommendation for me?"

"I was planning to do that later this week, after we finish the book."

"The book is done," Amy said. "It's been done for days. Nothing you do is going to make it any better."

"It still needs work."

"You're just dragging your feet."

"Why would I do that?"

"I don't know," she said with a shrug. "Maybe to keep me here."

Brendan stood up, then met her gaze mockingly. "Gee, I can't imagine why I'd want to do that. All we do is argue." He grabbed the manuscript pages from the sofa berth and tossed them on the table in the galley. "So you've decided to go to New York?"

"No," Amy said. "I'm just keeping my options open."

Brendan walked over to the Christmas tree and plucked at a piece of tangled tinsel. "You know, if you want to stay on the boat, you can. It might be nice to have someone here to keep an eye on things and it would give you a place to live until you figure out what you want to do. I wouldn't charge you any rent."

"I already know what I want to do," she said. She hesitated and he waited, holding his breath. "I was thinking I would take you up on your offer. I want to go to Turkey."

Brendan's head snapped around and he stared at her, wondering if he'd heard her right. "You're going to come with me?"

Amy shrugged, then rolled her eyes. "Yes, I'll come with you. But we're going to have to come to an understanding. I'm going for me, not for you. If I get over there and you don't need an assistant, I'm going to leave. I'll pay for my own ticket out of my salary."

Brendan crossed the cabin in a few long strides, then grabbed her around the waist and gave her a hug. "Things will work out," he said.

"But if they don't, if you decide that you don't want me there, I'll leave. And if I decide I don't want to be there, I'll leave. No strings, no commitments, no hard feelings. On either side."

Though Brendan wasn't crazy about the terms, he was willing to accept just about anything to keep Amy with him. He could change her mind later. They had more time and that's all he really needed to work everything out between them.

"There is one problem, though," she added.

"What's that?"

"My passport. It's at my parents' house. When I left, I never thought of taking it with me. I'm going to have to call them and tell them where I'm going. I'm going to have to convince them to send it to me. They could be really awful about this and keep it."

"Would they do that?"

Amy nodded. "They sent private detectives after me." She paused. "But there may be a way. I might be able to convince our housekeeper, Hannah, to get it out of my room and mail it to me."

"If she doesn't, we'll just get you another passport," Brendan said. "I'll call my agent and have him figure out what we need to do." He grabbed her around the waist and picked her up, hugging her hard. "We're going to have such a good time."

Amy braced her hands on his shoulders and looked down at him, a teasing grin quirking her lips. "We still haven't discussed my salary," she teased.

"We'll discuss that later. Now that you've decided to go, we need to get my manuscript printed out and sent to my editor. Then we need to get a visa for you and we'll need to go shopping for some clothes. You'll need a good pair of boots and some things comfortable enough to wear on an archaeological dig."

Brendan lowered her to her feet, letting her body slide along his. Then he grabbed her face between his hands and kissed her hard. He felt as if he'd rescued them both from the jaws of death. They'd have four whole months together, four more months to convince her that they could make it work, four months to make her fall in love with him.

Suddenly, all the problems that had rained down on

top of them had disappeared and life was simple again. It was just him and Amy. And that was exactly the way it was meant to be.

ruc to them had disappeared and life was simple again. It was instinctual and caring. And that was exactly the way Amy meant it to

8

AMY STARED at Brendan's cell phone, running her fingers over the buttons as she decided how she wanted to proceed. Her father would likely be at work. He always left the house before seven. And she was counting on her mother to be occupied with one of her Monday morning charity meetings. She'd have plenty of time to convince Hannah of her plight. Her parents' phone number ran though her head over and over again.

With a soft curse, she punched it in, then waited for an answer on the other end. A familiar voice came on after three rings. "Sloane residence."

"Hannah?"

"Yes." The housekeeper paused and Amy could hear her draw a sharp breath. "Miss Amelia?"

Amy bit her bottom lip, tears suddenly pressing at the corners of her eyes. There was still an undeniable pull toward a voice she'd known since childhood. She'd worked so hard to build a new life and now she felt as if she were stepping right back into the old, giving up her hard-earned freedom. "It's me, Hannah," she said.

"Oh, my goodness, Miss Amelia. Just a second, let me get your mother. She's right here."

"No, no, no!" Amy cried. But in the background she

heard Hannah calling her mother's name. Amy's finger hovered over the button, ready to end the call. A few seconds later, Dinah Sloane came on the line.

"Amelia? Amelia, darling, where are you? Don't hang up. I just want to talk to you. Darling, we've missed you. We've been so worried. Are you all right?"

Amy figured she'd have to talk fast. Knowing her father's determination to find her, he probably was tracing every call. "I'm fine, Mother. I just called to tell you that you don't have to worry about me. I'm doing really well."

"We've all been worried, dear. Especially Craig. He's—"

"Mother, I'm not going to marry Craig. I don't love him. I know you do, but I don't. So let's just get that straight between us right now."

"Darling, just come home," her mother begged. "We'll work everything out. We can't have Christmas without you. And your grandmother needs to see you. She's been ill lately and we're not sure whether she'll have another Christmas with us."

The news was like a slap to her face, stealing her breath and stopping her heart. "Grandmother is sick?" Amy tried to draw another breath but felt as if a two-ton weight were crushing her chest. "What's wrong with her?"

"Some kind of attack. The doctors think it was her heart. She's not doing well. She needs you, darling."

Amy knew she had to hang up soon. "I—I don't know, Mother. Maybe I'll come home. I—I just don't know. I'll call you again." With trembling fingers, she shut off the cell phone and set it down in front of her, as if just touching it burned her fingers. So much for getting her passport. She couldn't even think about going to Turkey now.

She rubbed her forehead with her fingers, trying to put her options in order. It wouldn't be beyond her parents to use her eighty-year-old grandmother in their scheme to get her back home. But there was only one way to really know. Amy pushed up from the table and hurried back to her cabin. She grabbed her suitcase and threw it open on her berth, then tiptoed into Brendan's cabin to collect her things. He was still asleep, his arms thrown out to his sides, his hair mussed, the twisted sheet revealing a naked hip and a muscular flank.

Amy bent down and gathered her clothes scattered across the floor. Then she plucked her watch from the bedside table and quickly tiptoed back out to her own cabin. She wasn't sure how long she'd be gone, but she threw in enough to last her for a few nights—makeup, toothbrush, clean underwear. Then she opened the drawer beneath her berth and pulled out her wallet from the place where she'd once hidden it from Brendan. She had over one hundred dollars in cash. That should be enough for the train to Boston, taxis and a cheap motel room for the night.

Amy quickly pulled on her clothes, then shoved the money into her jeans pocket. She snapped her suitcase shut and turned to the door, only to find Brendan standing there, watching her with undisguised curiosity.

"What's going on?" he asked, rubbing the sleep

from his eyes. He had dressed in a pair of baggy sweat-pants and socks, his chest still bare.

"I—I have to go," Amy said, squeezing past him, her suitcase clutched in her hands.

"Go where?"

"To Boston. I have something I have to do."

Brendan followed her out to the main cabin. "What do you have to do? Are you going to get your pass-port?"

"No," Amy said, searching for her purse in the main cabin. "It's my grandmother. She's sick. I have to see her. I have to make sure she's all right."

Brendan frowned, then glanced at the clock on the wall. "I'll go with you. I'll drive. I can be ready in a few minutes and we'll go together."

Amy shook her head. "No. I have to go on my own."

"When will you be back?" Brendan asked.

"I don't know," she replied, snatching up her jacket and finding her purse underneath.

"You are coming back, aren't you?" he asked.

Amy walked to the steps up to the deck, then turned and faced him. "I don't know. I won't know anything until I see her."

Brendan cursed softly, then crossed the cabin and grabbed her face between his palms, forcing her gaze to meet his. "I'm not going to let you go." He bent close and brushed a kiss across her lips. "You can't just walk out of here like this. What if you don't come back?"

"I have to go," Amy said.

"Why? So you can be pulled back to your old life? You have a life here with me. We belong together."

"If something happened to my grandmother and I

hadn't taken the chance to talk to her again, I'd never forgive myself. All my life I've looked up to her. I need to let her know how things turned out. I need to show her that I'm all right."

Brendan stared at her for a long moment. Then his expression softened. "At least let me drive you to the train station. I'll be dressed in just a few minutes, I swear."

He strode back to his cabin and Amy stood frozen in place, waiting for him to return. She glanced around, taking in her surroundings and trying to memorize every detail. A strange sense of forboding came over her and for a moment, she felt as if she might never see this place again.

Brendan reappeared and grabbed her suitcase from her hand. He helped her up the steps and out onto the deck, then shut the hatch behind them. Amy wanted to stop, to take another look around, to draw a long breath of the salty sea air, to listen to the clank of the rigging just once more, to step into his arms and feel the warmth of his embrace. Instead, she silently reassured herself that she would be coming back. She and Brendan would see each other again and they would go to Turkey together. Nothing would change.

Brendan jumped down to the dock then reached up to grab her waist. As he set her down on her feet, Amy pressed her palms against his chest. She hadn't even left yet and already an ache of loneliness grew in her heart. Just one night away, sleeping without him, waking up alone, seemed like an eternity.

She quickly pulled out of his embrace and started down the dock. Brendan caught up with her and grabbed her hand, lacing his fingers through hers. "Are you sure you don't want me to drive you into Boston?"

"You have to get your manuscript ready," she said. "And you've got all those things to do before you leave."

He yanked her to a stop, spinning her around to face him. "Before *we* leave."

She nodded. "Right. Before we leave."

When they reached the car, Brendan threw her bag in the back seat then pulled open her door. Amy settled herself inside, clutching her hands in front of her and trying to calm her jangled nerves. She felt as if she were being torn in two. She had to see her grandmother, yet she was terrified that the instant she set foot in her old world, she'd get drawn back in, caught in a web of guilt and family obligation that she couldn't escape.

The ride to the train station took just a few minutes and when they got out of the car, Amy saw a south-bound train approaching on the tracks. She and Brendan hurried inside the station and bought her a ticket on the next train to Boston, departing in just five minutes. They silently walked to the platform and Brendan set her suitcase down between them.

"Are you sure you'll be all right?" he asked.

Amy nodded. "If I'm lucky I'll be able to see my grandmother without my parents even knowing. She has a house on Beacon Hill. I just hope she's there and not in the hospital."

The train whistle split the crisp morning air, causing Amy to jump. The rumble grew louder and she reached down to grab her suitcase, but Brendan covered her hand with his, then drew her back up. He stared down into her eyes and pressed her fingers to his lips. "Amy, I have to tell you something."

She glanced over his shoulder at the approaching train, barely able to hear what he was saying. "What?"

"I love you," he shouted as the train squealed to a stop. "I want you to know that. I love you."

Amy wasn't sure she heard right and stepped closer. "What?"

"I love you," he repeated. He drew her into his arms and kissed her long and hard, as if to seal his words in her heart and in her mind. Then he grabbed her suitcase and walked with her toward the train. She hopped onboard and the conductor handed her suitcase up to her, then jumped on after her.

She stood in the doorway of the train and watched Brendan, her gaze flitting over his features, trying to make one last memory for herself. He looked just as he had the night she met him, his hair windblown, the dark shadow of a beard on his handsome face, and those beautiful golden-green eyes with the impossibly long lashes. Her breath caught in her throat as the conductor reached around her to close the door.

Brendan held up his hand to wave and she took a step forward. And then the words came, as natural as taking a breath and letting it out. "I love you," Amy called as the door closed. "I love you, Brendan Quinn."

She watched him through the window until the train began to move. Then he disappeared from view and Amy felt more alone than she'd ever felt in her life. She pressed her palm to her chest and tried to keep from bursting into tears. Brendan Quinn loved her. Now that he'd said the words, she wasn't quite sure what to do with them.

Amy turned to pick up her suitcase only to find the conductor holding it for her. He gave her a smile, then opened the door into the car. He followed her inside, then hefted her suitcase up onto the rack above her head. "Have a nice trip, miss," he said.

She forced a smile. "I'll try."

BRENDAN STOOD across the street from Quinn's Pub and stared at the building through the softly falling snow. Neon beer signs blazed in the plate glass windows and the sound of an Irish band drifted out every time the door opened. It was a Thursday night and the place would be packed. Two of his brothers would be behind the bar and no doubt, a few other Quinns would be sitting around, enjoying a pint or two of Guinness.

He reached in his pocket for his cell phone, then pulled it out and checked to see that the battery was charged. Over the past three days, he felt as if the phone had become a lifeline, something to hold onto when he had nothing else.

He'd waited for her to call that first night, certain that once she got settled she'd let him know how things were going. When she hadn't called by the next afternoon, he'd begun to worry. By the next day, Brendan had wondered if she'd call at all.

He'd waited around *The Mighty Quinn*, pacing the cabin until he couldn't stand it anymore, then decided to head into Boston to his father's pub. He'd left a note on the galley table with his whereabouts and instructions to call him immediately if she returned.

As he'd driven in, Brendan had thought about bypassing the pub and going to find Amy. The location of the Sloane mansion wasn't a secret. And she had mentioned that her grandmother lived on Beacon Hill. How many Aldrichs could there be living in such a small area? He'd knock on every door until he found the right one.

But in truth, Brendan was afraid that she'd decided not to come back. That by not contacting him she was sending an unspoken message that things were over between them. His thoughts jumped back to the morning at the train station. He'd admitted his love for her and she'd returned the sentiment. But if she really loved him, why hadn't she called? He was due to leave for Turkey in just four days. Time was running out.

"Give her another day," Brendan muttered. "You can always go find her tomorrow."

Brendan set off across the street and when he reached the pub door, he pulled it open and stepped inside. Though the atmosphere usually cheered him up, tonight the noise of the crowd and the music was grating on his ears. He spotted an empty stool near the end of the bar, then sat down.

A few seconds later, Conor came up and tossed a coaster in front of him. "What are you doing here?"

"Can't I stop by for a beer when I feel like it?" Brendan asked.

Conor glanced around "Where's Amy? Did you bring her along?"

Brendan shook his head and Conor gave him a shrewd look.

"What's wrong?" he asked.

"Nothing," Brendan replied. He turned his gaze to the rest of the bar, searching for a change of topic. A few stools away, at the waitress station, he saw a petite brunette he thought he recognized. He stared at her for a long moment, taking in her waifish figure and her short, shaggy haircut and the stylish tinted glasses she wore. "New waitress?" he asked.

Conor looked over and they both watched her as Liam loaded her tray with drinks. Brendan was certain he recognized her.

"Her name is Keely Smith. Liam hired her. She's not a great waitress, but she's easy on the eyes."

"I've seen her around," Brendan said. "Is she from the neighborhood?"

"I don't think so. She used to hang out here at the pub and then when we posted a sign for a new waitress, she asked for the job. I think she might be in love with Brian. That's why she took the job." Conor gave him a poke in the shoulder. "Did you really come in here to size up the waitresses?"

Brendan shook his head. "Nope. Give me a pint of Guinness."

Conor drew the dark brown beer from a tap at the middle of the bar, then set the glass in front of Brendan. "You know, we bartenders have a knack for sorting out problems. And I know you've got problems, boyo, from that hangdog look on your face."

Brendan took a long sip of his Guinness, then licked his upper lip. "She's gone," he said.

"Amy?"

Brendan nodded. "She left the day before yesterday. She found out her grandmother is ill. She hasn't called, hasn't tried to contact me and I'm beginning to believe she won't. We're supposed to leave for Turkey in four days."

"You're going to Turkey for Christmas?"

"For a job."

Conor shook his head. "I figured you'd be spending Christmas with the family. Olivia and Meggie have a big celebration planned. They wanted the whole family there. Olivia's going to be disappointed."

Brendan shrugged, then reached in his jacket pocket and pulled out the two presents he'd purchased at the gift shop in Gloucester. "Here. Put these under the tree. Hopefully, this will make up for my absence."

"You bought Olivia a present?"

"Meggie, too," Brendan said. "Earrings made of sea glass. Amy helped me pick them out."

Conor seemed impressed. "Earrings. Good choice."

"Yeah, good choice." Brendan nodded. "You know, I never wanted to fall in love with her. I did my best to avoid it. And then, I finally admit that I do love her and she walks out."

"Go get her," Conor said.

"Yeah, right. Just show up at the front door of the mansion and tell Avery Aldrich Sloane that I want to marry his daughter."

"You want to marry her?" Conor asked.

"Eventually. Isn't that what people in love do?"

Conor chuckled then waved to Liam at the end of the bar. "Brendan's gettin' married," he called. A few seconds later, Liam joined them. Then Dylan appeared from the crowd. Brendan waited for the twins, but Conor informed him that they both had dates and wouldn't be privy to the good news until later.

"Don't you think you're jumping the gun, Con," Brendan said. "She walked out on me. How the hell am I going to get her to marry me after that?"

"When are we going to meet her?" Dylan asked. "Why didn't you bring her along tonight?"

"She's...busy," Brendan said.

"Not too busy, I think," Conor replied. He cocked his head in the direction of the door and Brendan slowly turned. His breath caught in his throat as his gaze fell on her pretty face. He pushed away from the bar and quickly hurried toward her. "Amy. What are you doing here?" He grabbed her hands and gave them a squeeze.

"I stopped at the boat and found your note. We have to talk," she murmured, glancing around nervously.

Brendan looked over his shoulder at the raucous crowd. It was too noisy inside. "Outside," he said.

As they stepped out of the door, he couldn't help but notice the Bentley double-parked out in front. "Is that yours?" he asked.

"My grandmother's. My father gave it to her. She doesn't drive, so this is the only car she has."

Brendan chuckled. "You drove a Bentley to South Boston?"

"No, my grandmother's chauffeur drove. I rode in the back."

"Did you bring your things? Or did you drop them

at the boat? You got your passport from your parents' house, didn't you?"

Amy chewed on her bottom lip as she gazed up at him. "That's what I came here for. I wanted to say goodbye. I can't go with you, Brendan."

He stared down at her, taking in her uneasy expression, the way she clutched her hands in front of her, the indecision that haunted her blue eyes. "What are you saying?"

"I have to stay here. My grandmother needs me."

"No," Brendan said. "We were going together."

"And now you'll go alone." She drew a shaky breath. "We both knew this wouldn't work out, Brendan. There are too many complications—your career, my family. We want different things from life."

"We wanted the same things up until a few days ago. We wanted to be together, to be happy. When did that change?"

"We were living in a little fantasy world on *The Mighty Quinn*. You never needed an assistant, you were just making a job for me. And I don't really need a job. In a few months, I'll have a couple million dollars. I'll be able to buy anything I want."

"If that's what you wanted, then why did you run away in the first place? And why did you stay with me?"

"I thought I could become someone different. And for awhile, I did. But then I realized that no matter how much I'd like to pretend I'm just a regular person, it won't work. It's always there, all those millions defining who I am and what I should be."

"I can't give you anything you can't give yourself,"

Brendan said. "Except the promise that I'll always be there for you."

Amy smiled. "I know. And I understand how difficult that is." She reached up and touched his cheek. "But, we had a good time. And I'll never forget what you've done for me. You were there when I didn't have any place else to go. You gave me a chance to see that I could be my own person. That I was someone beyond Amelia Aldrich Sloane."

Brendan took her face between his hands and then touched her lips with his, a kiss so gentle and so stirring that he didn't want it to end. But she pulled away, her face flushed, her hands trembling. "Come with me," he said.

"I can't," she murmured.

"But I love you," he said, staring deep into her eyes.

Tears swam in her eyes and one trickled down her cheek. Brendan caught it with his thumb. "And I love you," she said with a wavering smile. "But that's not going to be enough. Maybe someday, I'll think back on this time and regret that I didn't go with you. But I don't ever want you to regret what we shared. And if we stay together, I think you might."

"I wouldn't," Brendan said. "Never."

Amy reached up and ran her fingers over his lips. She gave him a tremulous smile, one that said she didn't believe his words. Then she gave him a quick kiss before she turned and ran to the car. She hopped inside without even looking back.

Brendan wasn't sure how long he stood outside the bar, how many patrons walked past him, wondering what he was staring at down the long dark empty street. He finally moved when the cold began to seep through his clothes and the ache in his heart was too much to bear.

This couldn't be the end of it, so sudden and without a fight. He couldn't allow her to walk out of his life with barely a reasonable explanation. People in love were supposed to stay together forever, weren't they? With a low curse, he strode across the street to his car and got inside. But before he turned the ignition, he waited for the anger to subside.

"I never wanted this in the first place," Brendan muttered. "So why should I care? I'll go to Turkey and I'll forget all about her."

But as he pulled out into the street and drove away, Brendan knew that falling out of love with Amy Aldrich would be as difficult as it was to keep from loving her. She'd made a place for herself in his heart and removing her might just cost him a life that, until a few weeks ago, he'd never even believed possible.

"How are you feeling today, Grandmother?" Amy slipped through the bedroom door with the silver tray clutched in her hands. She smiled when she saw her grandmother sitting up in bed reading a magazine.

"I'm feeling just fine. I think it's time I got off my duff and got back to living. I hate lying around like I'm actually sick. I'm not, I tell you."

Amy sat down on the edge of the bed. Her grandmother certainly didn't look sick. Her youthful skin had a rosy glow and her gray hair, recently styled by a visit from the hairdresser, made her look as if she was ready to go out to lunch with some of her friends. "The doctor said you need to rest. You can get up tomorrow for a few hours but it's going to be awhile before you're going to be back to your regular schedule."

"Well, at least you should get back to your life," Adele Aldrich said. "You shouldn't be spending your days taking care of an old lady."

"You're not old. You're my grandmother. And I don't think there's a younger eighty-year-old woman in all of New England."

Her grandmother patted Amy's hand. "Sit here with me, darling, and have a cup of tea."

Amy did as she was told, reaching for the tray on the bedside table. She poured a cup and handed it to her grandmother. "I'm so glad you're feeling better. I was really worried."

"And I was worried about you," her grandmother said. "I didn't think that all our talk about adventure would send you running." Adele stared at her from above the rim of her teacup. "I feel as if I'm to blame."

"You told me to take my life into my own hands," Amy said, "and that's what I did."

Her grandmother took another sip of her tea, then set the cup down in the saucer. "So if you had a wonderful adventure, then why do you look so sad, Amelia? Give me a nice smile and tell me what you've been up to."

Amy laughed softly. "Well, I've had a lot of different jobs. And lived in some interesting places." She paused, pressing back a flood of emotion. "And I fell in love."

Grandmother Aldrich's eyebrow arched. "Ah, you

fell in love. Well that explains the sad face. Would you like to tell me about it?"

"It was wonderful. He was so sweet and considerate and encouraging. He thought I was a waitress at a bar and it didn't make any difference to him. He loved me for the person I was, not for the money. He gave me a place to live and a job. He kept me safe."

"And what does this young man do?" Adele asked.

"Well, he doesn't live off a trust fund. He's a writer. I helped him with his book. I was his assistant."

"And how was the sex. Was it good?"

Amy gasped. "Grandmother! You can't ask that!"

"You know I have to ask. You and I have always been completely honest with each other. And I need to know these things to properly evaluate what you're telling me."

"You're just nosy. And if you must know, the sex was...incredible." She paused.

"Better than that stuffy old Craig?" she asked.

Amy giggled. "Oh my, yes."

Her grandmother folded her hands on her lap. "Good. I never liked that boy. He had shifty eyes and I don't like shifty eyes."

"I've spent my whole life being a good little girl, minding my parents, making them proud. But I had no idea who I was. I wasn't ready to get married and I think you knew that, didn't you."

Adele nodded. "And now you do know who you are, Amelia?"

"I think so. At least I'm a lot closer to knowing."

"And this man, this writer, is he responsible for this?"

"He is," Amy said. "With him I can be free. Nothing mattered except the two of us."

"And where is this wonderful man? Why haven't I met him?"

"He's in Turkey right now," Amy said, staring at her fingers as she twisted them together. "He left yesterday and he'll be there for four months. He asked me to go with him, but I said no."

"And why did you do that?"

"Lots of reasons," she said.

"I hope one of them wasn't me."

Amy gave her grandmother's hand a squeeze. "I had to come home once I heard you were ill."

"Now I'm better. So you can go to Turkey and be with your sweetheart."

"It's more complicated than that," Amy explained. "He's a proud man and I'll be a rich woman and sometimes the two don't mix. Daddy would never approve of him. I don't think Brendan's ever picked up a copy of the *Wall Street Journal.* He lives on an old fishing boat. He doesn't even own a suit."

"Oh, don't worry about your father. He's an old fuddy-duddy. I swear I can't believe I gave birth to him. I think there was a mix-up at the hospital. He doesn't have an ounce of adventure in his soul. And he's determined to squeeze the last bit out of you." Her grandmother pointed to a table near the window. "Get my album," she said.

Amy walked to the table and picked up an elegant leatherbound picture album, brought it back and set it on her grandmother's lap. Adele opened it, then slowly flipped through the pages. She pointed to a picture of herself in a flying cap and leather jacket, a scarf rak-ishly tossed over her shoulder. "This was taken the day I soloed. My father was scandalized when I decided to learn how to fly. He thought it wasn't proper for a lady of my station. But all the boys were going off to war and I wanted to do something to help."

"You flew supply planes," Amy said.

"That's where I met your grandfather. He was an Air Force pilot and he was so handsome and charming. He swept me off my feet. And the sex was wonderful. Although, I must tell you, I didn't have anything to compare it to. Still, I knew."

"Sometimes, I think you were born in the wrong generation, Grandmother. You had a life of your own, you even kept your own name when you got married. You stood up to your father. And you were lucky enough to find a man who could handle who and what you were."

"Your grandfather was as poor as a churchmouse when I met him and terribly proud. He wanted to come back home and move to California and become a cropduster. And I wanted to help him. I was deter-mined to have him and the life we planned, even though my father would hear nothing of it. But we made it work."

"How? Didn't he resent the money?"

"No. Because we didn't use the money. We lived on his salary and once I inherited, I started to give the money away. We did good deeds, Amelia, we helped people. We gave your father enough money to start his company and when your grandfather died, I used what I had to make a comfortable life for myself. So you see, it can be done, Amelia. You can make it work."

"Daddy would never let me give his money away."

"Darling, that money was mine in the first place. If you want to give it away, your father can't say a thing about it." She leaned forward and gave Amy a kiss on the cheek. "I had my adventures and now you go have yours, Amelia. Take a chance, risk your heart. Go to Turkey and find your man. Tell him how you feel."

"I don't know where he is."

"Your father has some very fine private detectives on his payroll. Now that you've got your trust fund, you can afford to hire them."

"But I don't have my trust fund."

"Yes, you do. I'm in charge of the trust and I've decided to change the terms. The money is yours, Amelia. Now you can go off and have all the adventures you want."

Amy reached out and hugged her grandmother. "Thank you. I won't disappoint you, Grandmother."

"You never have before and you never will. Just be yourself, darling and you'll have a happy life. And maybe, if you're lucky, you'll have a long time to live with your sweetheart and you'll give me many great-grandchildren."

9

THE SLOANE MANSION in Chestnut Hill was an aristo-
cratic property with a wide circular drive, an imposing
stone facade and gates to keep the riffraff out. Brendan
steered his car through the open gates and pulled to a
stop in front of the house. He peered through the frosty
windows of his car at the wide front door, draped with
elegant Christmas garland.

Reaching for the gearshift, he was ready to throw the
car into "drive" and make an escape. Instead, he
turned the ignition off, gave himself a silent pep talk
and got out of the car. As he walked to the front door,
he wasn't sure what he'd say. Hell, he wasn't even sure
Amy was here. All he knew was that when he'd
tracked down her grandmother's place on Beacon Hill,
the maid had informed him that both Adele and Amelia were at the family estate.

He chuckled softly, thinking of the old place on Kilgore Street as the Quinns' "family estate." How much
more would he have to learn about the fabulously
wealthy in order for him to understand Amy's way of
life? A huge brass door knocker adorned the front
door, but Brendan choose the little button at the side,
certain that the knocker was ornamental.

As he waited, he smoothed his hands over his jacket
and then ran his fingers through his windblown hair.

The door opened in front of him and an elderly woman in a black dress and white apron smiled in greeting. "May I help you?"

"I'd like to see Amy—I mean, Amelia Aldrich... Sloane."

The woman gave him the once-over, her gaze critically taking in every aspect of his appearance and making a judgement. "Then you must be him," she said.

"Him?"

"The one. The one who sent her running home. I guess we should thank you."

"Is Amy here?" Brendan asked.

She nodded curtly, then stepped aside to let him pass. He was barely inside when he was forced to stop and stare. The foyer was breathtaking with its cathedral ceiling dripping with Christmas decorations, fresh greenery, satin ribbon and what looked like real fruit. A huge tree stood in the corner, dwarfing the tree that Amy had put up on the boat. "Wow," he murmured.

"Come with me, please. Mr. Sloane will see you in the library."

"I didn't come here to see Mr. Sloane," Brendan said.

"Mr. Sloane sees all visitors," she said.

They wound through the main floor until they came to a panelled hallway near the rear of the house. The housekeeper knocked softly on a door, then stepped inside and murmured a few words to the room's occupant. More words were exchanged and then Brendan was motioned inside. He felt like a prisoner on the way to the gallows—or a kid standing outside the principal's office.

"Come in," the man behind the desk said. Avery Aldrich Sloane was of medium height with graying hair and wore impeccably pressed clothes. Sloane stood and held out his hand and Brendan reached out to shake it. "Avery Sloane."

"Brendan Quinn."

"Please, sit," he said, motioning to a leather wing-back chair. "You're here to see Amelia?"

Brendan nodded. "Is she here?"

"May I ask why you'd like to see her?"

"She and I are friends. You didn't answer my question. Is she here?"

"You're the writer, then. The one who lives on the boat."

Brendan was getting a bit tired of the runaround. "Either she's here or not," he said. "If she's not, then I'll just be going."

"She's here," Sloane said. "But I don't know if she wants to see you."

"Don't you think we should let her decide that?"

"Amy doesn't always know what's best for herself," Sloane said.

Brendan cursed softly, then stood up and leaned over Sloane's desk. He pressed his hands against the smooth mahogany and tried to school his temper. "With all due respect, Mr. Sloane, I don't think you know your daughter at all. She's beautiful and intelligent and determined to live her life the way she wants and that's what I admire about her. You can't make her be something she doesn't want to be. Sooner or later, she'll run again. And I might not be there to keep her safe. I don't think either one of us wants that, do we?"

Sloane stared at him for a long moment, then nodded. "You look like a reasonable man," he said. He reached into the top drawer of his desk and pulled out a large book. When he flipped it open, Brendan saw that it was a checkbook, one of those that only businesses and very wealthy people used. Sloane grabbed a pen from the desk set and scribbled something on one of the checks, then held it out to Brendan.

"I didn't come here for money," Brendan said. "I came here to find Amy. That's all. I just need to talk to her."

"And you will." He waved the check. "Go ahead. Take it."

"I'm not going away just because you pay me."

"I'm not paying you to go away," Sloane said. "I want you to marry my daughter."

Brendan gasped. "What?"

"This is a dowry, of sorts. You take it and she's yours."

"You want me to marry Amy?"

"For some strange reason she fancies herself madly in love with you. Her grandmother has informed me that if I stand in the way of this union, then she'll make my life a living hell. I love my mother dearly and one of the qualities that I love the most about her is that she is a woman of her word. I've tried my best to make her see reason, but she won't be happy unless Amelia marries you. Now, I don't want you to tell Amelia that we had this conversation. If she thinks I approve then she'll drop you in an instant. She's developed a rather rebellious streak."

Brendan took the check from his fingers, his eyes widening at the number of zeros. This was what he wanted, but he wasn't sure whether he'd just been handed the greatest gift in the world or whether Sloane had manipulated him into doing his dirty work. Brendan handed the check back to Sloane. "You can keep your money," he said.

"You're not going to marry her?" Sloane sighed. "I suppose I could try to force you."

"That won't be necessary. I don't need money to love your daughter. I can do that all on my own. I can also propose on my own—if that's what I choose to do." He paused. "I appreciate your blessing, sir, strange as it is. And I thank you for your support."

"Don't thank me," Sloane said. "You still have to convince Amelia." He nodded toward the door. "She's upstairs visiting with her grandmother."

Brendan walked to the door, but Sloane's voice stopped him. "One more thing," he said. Brendan turned just as he tossed a small velvet pouch across the room. Inside was a beautiful diamond ring. "It's a family heirloom. Amelia's grandmother would like her to have it." He held up his hand. "I'm not saying you can't afford to buy your own. It's just tradition and I'm sure it would mean a lot to Amelia."

Brendan stared down at the ring, then nodded. "Thanks," he said.

He hurried out of the library and wound his way back to the foyer and up the sweeping staircase to the second floor. He took the stairs two at a time but when he reached the top he was faced with a long hallway and multiple doors. An elderly woman stepped out of a door near the end of the hall and Brendan approached her.

"I'm looking for Amelia," he said. "Do you know where she is?"

The woman smiled, smoothing her hands over her trim suit. "You must be Brendan." She held out her hand. "I'm Amelia's grandmother, Adele Aldrich. I understand your sister-in-law is Olivia Farrell. Olivia and I are great friends. Why just yesterday, she called me about an Empire-style writing desk that she found. She thought it would be perfect for my—" The woman stopped, then gave him an apologetic smile. "Come with me," she said. "You and I have to have a little talk."

"I'd really like to see Amy," Brendan said.

"This will only take a few minutes."

Brendan followed her down the hall to another room, wondering if Amy was even in the house and if he'd ever get to see her. He entered yet another elegant room, a bedroom this time with a huge sitting area and a fireplace near the tall windows. Adele sat down and Brendan took the chair across from her.

"I suppose you've spoken to Amelia's father. He's indicated that the family would support a match between you two. Of course, he probably didn't outline the conditions of our support."

Brendan held out his hand and stood. "Listen, I don't need to discuss conditions, I need to—"

"Sit down," Adele commanded, in a voice that was both perfectly polite and imperiously demanding. Brendan had no choice but to follow her order. "Well, that's better. Now, here are my conditions. First of all, you better be damn sure you're marrying her for the right reasons, Mr. Quinn. Amelia can be a headstrong and rebellious girl and if you think to change her once she's your wife, I can tell you, it won't work."

"I'd never try to change her. That's what I love about her."

"Good," Adele said. "Second, Amelia can make some rather rash decisions in her life. She doesn't always look before she leaps. You must promise to always keep her best interests at heart and to try to modify this behavior when personal safety is a concern."

"I understand," Brendan said, thinking back to her leap into the Gloucester harbor.

"And finally, there is the matter of children. I want great-grandchildren quickly and in large quantities."

Brendan chuckled. "I think that would have to be up to Amy. Although I do want children, I—" He paused. "I think we're getting a little ahead of ourselves here. Amy and I haven't even discussed marriage. I'm not even sure she's going to want to see me."

Adele smiled. "She's in the room at the end of the hall." She held out her hand and Brendan helped her up from her chair. Then to his surprise, she pushed up on her toes and kissed his cheek. "You remind me of my Richard," she murmured. "We had a happy life together and that's really all I wish for Amelia."

"I'll try my best," Brendan said.

"Then go," Adele said, shooing him away with her hand. "Go find your Amy."

Brendan hurried out of the room and down the hall, but when he knocked on the last door, there was no answer. He peeked inside to find the room empty. He was about to pay another visit to Adele when he heard footsteps on the stairs. He slowly turned, then froze.

AMY STOOD in the hallway, her hand gripping the banister, her heart slamming in her chest. It had only been a few days since she'd last seen him, yet it seemed like forever. What was he doing here? She wanted to run to him and throw herself into his arms, to smooth her fingers over his face and to taste his lips, but she held back, not sure why he'd come.

She watched as his gaze took in her appearance. Amy knew she looked different. Her hair was back to its original color and pulled into a sleek ponytail. And her multiple earrings were gone. She wore a simple cashmere sweater and a pair of tailored trousers. She didn't look anything like the girl he'd rescued from the Longliner. Except that she wore the sea glass pendant he'd given her. She reached for it now, fingering it nervously. "You're here," she said.

"I am," Brendan replied, taking a step toward her.

His voice, so deep and warm, sent a flood of desire racing through her bloodstream. She remembered that voice whispering in her ear, saying her name as they made love. She swallowed hard. "But you're supposed to be in Turkey. You were supposed to leave yesterday."

"I postponed my trip," Brendan said. "I wanted to spend Christmas in Boston. So, how are you, Amy?"

"I'm fine," she said.

He took another step. "You look...different. Beautiful," he added. "But different."

Amy reached up and touched her hair. "My mother

just kept harping on the blond so I thought it would be easier just to change it back."

He reached out, as if to touch her hair, but then pulled his hand back. "I like it," Brendan said. "But I liked the other color, too."

"Why haven't you left?" Amy asked moving to sit on the low sofa near the landing windows. Her knees were already wobbly and she wasn't sure how much longer she could stand.

He sat down beside her. "I wasn't ready. I needed to talk to you. We didn't get a chance to talk much that night at the pub. And there's a lot left to be said."

"Is there?"

He nodded, then reached out and grabbed her fingers. "I met your father. We had an...interesting conversation."

Amy felt her cheeks warm with embarrassment. Knowing her father, he did all the talking and Brendan was expected to listen obediently. "I can just imagine what he had to say to you. I'm sorry. He had no right to speak to you like that."

"I don't think you can imagine what he said. Or did. He handed me a check—a very *big* check. At first I figured he wanted to get rid of me. But then he said the check was a dowry. It seems your father wants me to marry you. And your grandmother concurs."

Amy gasped. "Marry me?"

"Your grandmother and I had a very nice little chat. She's an incredible, lady, Amy."

Amy stood up and began to pace in front of the sofa, unable to believe what she was hearing. "They want *you* to marry *me*."

Brendan nodded. "I think your father believes if he says you should marry me, you'll do the opposite. And your grandmother has convinced him that I'd be the man for the job."

Amy felt her mortification slowly dissolve into anger. She clenched her fists at her side and cursed softly. They'd planned her whole life out for her, her father, her grandmother and even Brendan. This was exactly what had happened with Craig! "The man for the job," Amy repeated softly. She turned on him. "And what job is that? Training me to become a dutiful wife and doting mother?"

The bitterness in her words took him by surprise. "Amy, I—"

"Don't say another word!" she warned. "I can't believe you. You're siding with them. They've completely manipulated you and you let them! I thought you were stronger than that. I—I thought you were different."

Brendan stood and grabbed her arm, then turned her toward him. "I didn't let them manipulate me. I listened to what they had to say and that's all. I came here because I want us to have a life together. I came here because I realize I can't live another day without you. And usually, when a guy feels that strongly, he asks the woman he loves to marry him. So, will you marry me, damn it?"

"Oh, now there was a heartfelt proposal," she said with a dismissive laugh. "I suppose now I should get all teary-eyed and profess my undying devotion to you."

Brendan reached into his pocket and withdrew a

small velvet pouch. He fumbled with the string, then pulled out a ring—her grandmother's diamond ring! She could see the frustration in his eyes as he held it out to her. "Before you get all misty," he said, a sarcastic edge to his voice, "let me do this right. Amy, I love you. I've loved you since the moment I carried you out of the Longliner. And I'll love you every day that I draw breath. Will you marry me?"

"Where did you get that ring?"

"Your father gave it to me. He thought you'd like to have it. Something about a family tradition." He grabbed her hand and pushed the ring onto her finger.

But Amy yanked it right back off and threw it at him. It dropped to the carpet at his feet. "That was the worst proposal I ever heard. And I won't marry you. Not now, not ever."

"You know, this is exactly what your father wanted. He said you'd do this and he had you pegged. I think you're the one being manipulated here."

Amy shook her head. "Just go away," she murmured. "I don't want to hear any more. I wish I'd never met you."

"I'm not going away," he said. "I love you and I know you love me. We belong together."

"You make it sound so simple," she said.

"It is simple. It has been from the start. All you have to do is think about you and me. Forget everything else." Brendan reached out and took her face between his palms, refusing to let her go when she tried to pull away. He met her gaze and for a moment, she went still. Then he pressed a soft kiss to her mouth. "See. That was simple. Just you and me."

"Kiss me again," she said.

"No, you kiss me."

With a soft curse, she grabbed his face and pressed her lips to his, only this time, she lingered a bit longer, their tongues softly touching and tasting. He moaned and a shiver ran through her. Why was she fighting him? She knew she loved Brendan. And she wanted to spend the rest of her life with him.

Amy sighed. "All right," she said. "I'll marry you."

Brendan stepped back, staring at her in disbelief. "You will?"

"Yes," Amy said. "But you have to work up a better proposal. That just wasn't romantic at all. You can do better."

Brendan reached down to the floor and grabbed the ring. "You aren't kidding, are you? You really want to marry me?"

"That's not good enough. You're supposed to get down on your knee."

"Are you editing my prose again?" he asked.

"Sorry," Amy said with a giggle. "Force of habit. But I want a proposal that I can tell everyone about. Not just, 'Marry me, damn it.'"

"All right, all right," Brendan said. He pulled her along to the sofa and gently pushed her down. Then he knelt in front of her on one knee and held her fingers between his hands. "When I met you, Amy Aldrich, I didn't want to fall in love. But with every day that passed, I realized that I couldn't stop myself. There was a reason I was sitting in the Longliner that night and it wasn't to get another interview or to soak up the atmosphere. It was you. I was meant to be there for you." Brendan bent and kissed her fingertips, then slowly slid the ring onto her finger. "I believe that great Irish poet Dermot Quinn said, 'Grow old along with me, the best is yet to be.'"

"That was Robert Browning," Amy corrected. "And he wasn't even Irish."

"You're editing again," Brendan warned.

Amy laughed. "Sorry. Go on."

Brendan shrugged. "There's no more. Marry me, Amy Aldrich Sloane. Grow old with me and I promise you that life will be one long and glorious adventure that we'll experience together."

Amy slipped her arms around his neck, then knelt down on the floor beside him, staring into his eyes. "I will marry you," she said. With a tiny cry of delight, she kissed him as they both tumbled to the floor.

Brendan pulled Amy on top of him and they were lying on the oriental carpet, kissing passionately when her grandmother walked through. "Amelia?"

Amy looked up and smiled, then brushed a strand of hair from her eyes. "Yes, Grandmother."

"Is this proper behavior for a young woman of your background?"

Amy held out her hand, the diamond glinting in the soft light from the windows. "We're engaged," she said. "Brendan and I are getting married."

A slow smile grew on Adele Aldrich's face and she nodded. "Well then," she said. "Please, carry on."

Brendan growled softly, then pulled Amy back into a kiss that made her heart pound and her head spin. When she finally drew away and she looked down into his handsome face, she knew he'd spoken the truth.

Life with Brendan Quinn was bound to be the best adventure of all.

"You know, we're not going to be rich," she said.

His brow rose. "No?" he asked with a teasing smile. "I guess I'll learn to cope."

"I've decided to give it all away. I'm going to set up a foundation like my grandmother did. I'm going to do good deeds. And you can help me."

Brendan grabbed her around the waist, rolled her beneath him and kissed her again. "I'd like that," he said. "And you can help me edit my books."

"I'd like that," Amy said.

Brendan brushed the hair out of her eyes, then placed a kiss on the end of her nose. "We're going to be great together," he said.

"Yes, we are," Amy replied.

BY THE TIME they arrived at Quinn's Pub, the Christmas celebrations were in full swing. The pub stayed open until five on Christmas Eve and most of the regulars stopped by for free Guinness and a bowl of Irish stew. Brendan and Amy had promised to return to the Sloane mansion for her family's Christmas Eve dinner before coming back in to South Boston for midnight mass with the Quinns.

When they walked in, Dylan saw them first. "And there's the man of the hour," he shouted. "Come on, Bren, we've been waiting for you."

Brendan grabbed Amy's hand and drew her along toward a crowd of Quinns that included all his brothers, his father, Olivia, Meggie and Meggie's brother, Tommy.

"Well," Conor said, clapping Brendan on the back. "I see you survived that little problem and you're in good holiday spirits." He leaned closer. "Just find yourself another girl, that's the way."

Brendan laughed, then wrapped his arms around Amy's waist. "I'm afraid this is...or was, my problem. I think most of you know Amy. My fiancée?"

Those who had met her stared, mouths agape, both at her altered appearance and the news that she and Brendan were engaged. Then, Olivia jumped off her stool and wrapped Amy in a tight embrace. "I barely recognized you. Your hair, it's so different."

Meggie joined them, giving Amy a kiss on the cheek. "We're so glad you came. And so happy to hear your news."

Brendan stood back and watched as Amy was immediately accepted into the Quinn clan. Only Seamus stood back a bit, watching all the commotion as he sipped his Guinness. Brendan stepped to his side and wrapped his arm around his father's shoulders. "Well, Da," he said, loud enough for the others to hear. "What do you think?"

Seamus took another long sip of his beer, then slowly shook his head. "Ah, geez," he said, rubbing his hand on his chest. "Not another one. Have I taught you boys nothing? Our Quinn ancestors are rolling over in their graves, they are."

"You taught us well," Brendan said. "We just didn't listen. And since we seem to be going down in order, I guess Sean would be next, wouldn't he?"

"Oh, no," Sean said, holding out his hand. "You

won't get me to the altar. Besides, Brian is the older twin. He would be next."

"I am not," Brian protested. "Da, who's the oldest?"

"I don't remember," Seamus said. "The night you were born I was hoisting a few with my mates at the pub."

"When are you getting married?" Olivia asked.

"We were thinking about city hall, New Year's Eve day," Brendan said. "We leave for Turkey right after that and we'll probably have to come back and have a big society wedding for Amy's mother. Maybe in the fall."

"But you will be back in time for our wedding," Meggie said, concern etching her brow.

Amy nodded. "We're only going to stay in Turkey for three months instead of four. Brendan convinced his publisher that there's no reason to be there so long. We'll be back in plenty of time, I promise."

"Good," Meggie said. "Because you'll have to be a bridesmaid."

Amy's eyes went wide with surprise. "Me? You barely know me."

"You're going to be my sister-in-law. And I don't have any real sisters. Olivia has already agreed, so you have to say yes."

"Yes!" Amy cried, a smile breaking across her face. "Oh, and I can give you lots of advice for the wedding, since I've already planned and canceled one."

"But she's promised she won't be canceling the next one," Brendan added drawing her into a passionate kiss.

With that, the celebration began. There was laughing

and dancing and congratulations all around. Christmas music blared from the jukebox and bowls of hot Irish stew were served up with great fanfare. After a long time, Brendan managed to pull Amy away from the group and indulge in a long, lingering kiss near the pool table.

But Amy quickly pulled away. "Wait," she said. "I have something to give you." She hurried over to her bag and pulled out a thin, flat gift. When she returned to his side, she held it out to him.

"What's this?" Brendan asked.

"A present, silly. For you. Open it."

"Shouldn't we save it for later?"

Amy shook her head. "Now is the right time. It's the perfect time."

But they were interrupted when the pub's newest cocktail waitress appeared next to the pool table with a tray in her hands. She smiled shyly, avoiding their gazes. "Conor sent this over," she said, setting a champagne flute for each of them on the pool table. She handed Brendan the open bottle. "Congratulations," she murmured. "I hope you two will be very happy."

"Thank you," Brendan said, touched that a stranger would take such an interest in his announcement.

The waitress hurried away, but Amy stared after her, a frown wrinkling her brow. "Is she family?" she asked.

Brendan shook his head as he poured the champagne. "No."

"Hmm," Amy said. "She looks just like a Quinn, doesn't she? The dark hair and the eyes. Especially around the mouth. I just assumed she was a cousin."

She sighed softly, then turned back to Brendan, the waitress forgotten. "So open it," she said.

He set the champagne aside, then tugged off the ribbon and the heavy wrapping paper. "What is it?" he asked, shaking the box.

"You'll see."

He opened the top of the box to find a book. But it wasn't just any book. He read the title, elaborately hand-lettered in gold on the cover. "Legends of the Mighty Quinns," he murmured. Brendan opened the book, the pages made of thick paper. On the first page, he found a picture of a little boy sitting in a tree, a princess in a golden cage hanging beside him. "Tadleigh Quinn," he said, stunned.

He looked up at Amy and she smiled. "I changed the ending of the story to something a little happier. The princess is really a princess and she marries Tadleigh. I guess since I'm going to be a Quinn that's allowed, right?"

"You did this?" Brendan asked, flipping through the book, staring in wonder at the beautiful illustrations.

"The drawings. You did the stories."

"When did you have time? And where did you get such a talent?"

"I took a lot of art lessons as a child. Proper upbringing and all. And I worked on these on the boat late at night, after you went to sleep. And at home. I wanted to give you something for Christmas and since I didn't have any money at the time, I thought you might like this. I copied all the tales, just as you had written them. Except for Tadleigh, of course. That one I had to do by memory."

Brendan stared at the book, amazed at the way Amy had brought the characters in the Quinn stories to life. Fomor the giant and Odran Quinn. Eamon Quinn and his dragon. And Lorcan Quinn and the mermaid. "I don't know what to say," Brendan murmured, a surge of emotion tightening his throat. "No one's ever given me a gift like this."

"You like it then?" Amy asked.

Brendan reached out and pulled her into his embrace. "It's beautiful. It will be something we can share with our children." He wrapped his arms around her waist and bent to kiss her. As he lost himself in the taste and warmth of her mouth, he thought about the Mighty Quinns and the tales he'd been told as a child.

Someday he'd tell the tales to his own children, only they'd be tales of love and devotion and eternal happiness. He'd tell them about how the Mighty Brendan Quinn rescued the fair princess Amelia and how he spirited her away on his beautiful boat. How her father, the evil king, had offered a ransom for her return, but how Brendan refused him, believing that true love was all that mattered.

As Brendan drew back and looked down into Amy's face, he realized that this was no fairy tale. Brendan Quinn had found his true love and in the face of overwhelming odds, she had agreed to spend her life with him. As a boy, he'd listened to the tales of the Mighty Quinns and longed for adventure in faraway places. But as Amy's gaze met his, Brendan knew that the only place he wanted to be was in her arms and that the best adventure of his life was about to begin.

But the story's not over yet....
Who is the new waitress working at
Quinn's Pub?
What secret is she hiding?
And what does she want with the Quinn
family?
Find out in...
REUNITED
A Harlequin Single Title release
Available June 2002 wherever Harlequin
books are sold.
Watch for it!

CHAPTER ONE

A WIND-DRIVEN RAIN stung Keely McClain's face as she walked down the slick sidewalk, her hands shoved into her jacket pockets, her gaze fixed a few feet ahead of her. She was almost afraid to look up, afraid to face what she had come to see.

Keely had planned the trip to South Boston over and over again, first in her mind and then with maps spread out on her kitchen table, plotting how long it would take to drive from Brooklyn to Boston and back again, how far from the interstate she'd find Quinn's Pub, how the place would look once she finally set eyes on it.

All her planning had really been an attempt to avoid going in the first place. But the trip had been inevitable. And now that she was here, her only thought was how easy it would be to turn around and go home, to take the safe way out.

But curiosity drove her forward, in spite of her pounding heart and her quickened breathing. Maybe her mother had been right. Fiona McClain—Fiona *Quinn*—had begged her to wait before taking such a drastic step, but Keely knew her mother would only use the time to try to change her mind.

The past was the past, Fiona had said. *Leave it alone.*

The past that Keely had believed was *her* past had been nothing but a lie, a fabrication devised to quell a curious child's questions. The father she thought had died in a commercial fishing accident was really alive. And the siblings she'd always longed for were living in a city just a few hundred miles from her home in Brooklyn, living lives that she could only imagine. Keely drew a shaky breath, then turned and looked across the street.

It was there, right where it was supposed to be, neon beer signs blazing in the front windows. Quinn's Pub, owned by her father, Seamus Quinn, was typical of the bars in the neighborhood. "Seamus," she murmured. "Seamus, Conor, Dylan, Brendan, Sean, Brian, Liam."

Until a month ago, the names were those of strangers. But in just a few moments of shocking revelation in her grandmother's garden in Ireland, they'd become her family. Now, she repeated them over and over again like a mantra, hoping that the mere sound of the syllables would conjure up images of the men who went with the names.

She crossed the street, planning only to peek inside the wide plate glass windows and get a feel for the place. But as she approached the bar, a man pushed open the front door and stepped outside, then another right behind him. An Irish tune drifted into the cool October night from the interior of the pub. The lights flooding the front facade provided enough illumination for Keely to see both men, but her gaze was caught by the taller of the two.

He had to be one of her brothers, though she wasn't sure which one he was. The man's features were so unique, the dark hair, the strong jaw and the wide mouth, the very same features she looked at in the mirror every morning, hers softened to a feminine form. The same features she'd seen in the old photograph, now altered by age.

Keely had no choice but to continue walking. To turn and run would only draw attention to herself. As she passed the pair, she glanced up at the man and her gaze locked with his. The recognition she felt was reflected in his own expression and for a moment, Keely was sure he was going to stop and speak to her. A jolt of panic raced through her and she opened her mouth. But a casual greeting was too much. Instead, she just kept walking…walking until they were nearly face-to-face…walking until they had passed… walking until she felt a pang of regret at the missed opportunity.

"Keep walking," Keely murmured to herself. "Don't look back."

When she reached the front door of the pub, she started up the steps, but her courage had already been severely tested. If this was how she reacted to a stranger on the street—a stranger who might or might not be one of her brothers—then how would she react when she saw her father for the first time in her life?

Another wave of panic overwhelmed her and she spun on her heel and hurried back down the steps. She kept going until she reached the shadow of a panel truck parked along the curb. Then Keely turned and watched the two men as they got into an old car parked halfway down the block. Had the man recognized her the same way she'd recognized him? Had he seen the same family resemblance that she'd noticed?

The car pulled away from the curb and the two men drove past her. At the last second she stepped into the light. "Wait!" Keely called, raising her hand to wave at them.

But her voice caught in her throat and the word was barely more than a sigh. "Wait," she murmured as the taillights of the car disappeared into the rain and darkness. Keely stood on the sidewalk for a long time, letting the raindrops spatter on her face and the cold seep through her jacket.

A shiver skittered down her spine and Keely blinked, forced to admit that she had failed. With a softly muttered curse, she turned and started back in the direction from which she had come. When she reached the safety of her car, Keely closed her eyes and tipped her head back against the seat, trying to ignore her disappointment.

"That wasn't so bad," she murmured as her heart began to slow to its normal rhythm. "It was just a first step. The second will be much easier."

She flipped on the overhead light and grabbed her purse from the floor, then pulled out the tattered photograph. The color was faded but the images were still strong, an Irish family standing on an unknown bluff overlooking the Atlantic. The five boys were so young, Conor, the oldest, just seven or eight. Liam hadn't even been born yet, although Keely could detect the gentle swell of her mother's belly.

They all looked so happy, so hopeful, ready to set out on their grand adventure to America. Life was supposed to hold such promise, yet sometime in the following few years, it all went bad.

As Keely rubbed her thumb over the photo, she tried to imagine her mother in those days before she walked away from her family. The idea that her mother had left six sons behind was impossible to imagine. And though Keely had questioned her mother again and again, Fiona McClain had refused to provide an explanation, leaving Keely to wonder whether she had been the cause—or the pregnancy that resulted in her birth had been.

Slouching down in her seat, Keely turned her gaze toward the door of the pub, watching as patrons walked in and out, hoping that she'd see another man who resembled the boys in the picture. "Conor, Dylan, Brendan," she murmured. "Sean, Brian, Liam."

Who were they? What kind of men had they grown up to be? Were they kind and understanding, compassionate and open-minded? How would they react to her sudden appearance in their life? She'd grown up not knowing her brothers existed and Keely was certain they knew nothing of her. Would they accept her into the family or would they turn her away?

"Conor, Dylan, Brendan. Sean, Brian, Liam, Keely."

A tiny smiled curled the corners of her mouth. "Keely Quinn," she said. It sounded right. Though she'd spent her life calling herself Keely McClain,

Keely Quinn was her real name and it was time to start thinking of herself as a woman with real family—a father, a mother and six brothers.

She made a timetable for herself, a habit that was a necessity in her career and now came in handy in her personal life. In a few weeks, she'd come back to Quinn's Pub, walk inside and buy a drink. And a few weeks after that, maybe she'd speak to her father or one of her brothers. But before Christmas, Keely was determined that her family would know she existed. They didn't have to accept her at first. In truth, she didn't expect a tearful reunion and declarations of love. She expected shock and confusion and maybe a bit of resentment. But sooner or later, she would have the family that she always wanted.

With a soft sigh, Keely took a final look at the front door of Quinn's Pub then reached for the key in the ignition. But it was a long drive back to New York and she couldn't keep her news to herself. She reached into her purse and grabbed her cell phone, then punched in the phone number of her mother's house.

Fiona usually left the shop around six. By seven she was preparing her dinner and by eight, she had settled comfortably in her favorite chair with a mystery novel. Keely's mind raced as she tried to decide what she'd say. All she knew was that she had to hear her mother's voice, that calm, reassuring tone that always soothed her hurt and confusion. Her mother picked up the phone on the other end.

"Mama?" Keely said, her voice trembling. "Mama, I found them."

CALL THE ONES YOU LOVE OVER THE HOLIDAYS!

Save $25 off future book purchases when you buy any four Harlequin® or Silhouette® books in October, November and December 2001,

PLUS

receive a phone card good for 15 minutes of long-distance calls to anyone you want in North America!

WHAT AN INCREDIBLE DEAL!

Just fill out this form and attach 4 proofs of purchase (cash register receipts) from October, November and December 2001 books, and Harlequin Books will send you a coupon booklet worth a total savings of $25 off future purchases of Harlequin® and Silhouette® books, AND a 15-minute phone card to call the ones you love, anywhere in North America.

Please send this form, along with your cash register receipts
as proofs of purchase, to:
In the USA: Harlequin Books, P.O. Box 9057, Buffalo, NY 14269-9057
In Canada: Harlequin Books, P.O. Box 622, Fort Erie, Ontario L2A 5X3
Cash register receipts must be dated no later than December 31, 2001.
Limit of 1 coupon booklet and phone card per household.
Please allow 4-6 weeks for delivery.

**I accept your offer! Enclosed are 4 proofs of purchase.
Please send me my coupon booklet
and a 15-minute phone card:**

Name: _____

Address: _____ City: _____

State/Prov.: _____ Zip/Postal Code: _____

Account Number (if available): _____

---

097 KJB DAGL
PHQ4013

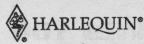

*H*ugh Blake, soon to become stepfather to the Maitland clan, has produced three high-performing offspring of his own. But at the rate they're going, they're never going to make him a grandpa!

There's *Suzanne*, a work-obsessed CEO whose Christmas spirit could use a little topping up....

And *Thomas*, a lawyer whose ability to hold on to the woman he loves is evaporating by the minute....

And *Diane*, a teacher so dedicated to her teenage students she hasn't noticed she's put her own life on hold.

But there's a Christmas wake-up call in store for the Blake siblings. Love *and* Christmas miracles are in store for all three!

Maitland Maternity Christmas

A collection from three of Harlequin's favorite authors

Muriel Jensen
Judy Christenberry
& Tina Leonard

Look for it in November 2001.

WITH HARLEQUIN AND SILHOUETTE

There's a romance to fit your every mood.

Passion

Harlequin Temptation

Harlequin Presents

Silhouette Desire

Pure Romance

Harlequin Romance

Silhouette Romance

Home & Family

Harlequin
American Romance

Silhouette
Special Edition

A Longer Story With More

Harlequin
Superromance

Suspense & Adventure

Harlequin Intrigue

Silhouette Intimate
Moments

Humor

Harlequin Duets

Historical

Harlequin Historicals

Special Releases

Other great
romances
to explore

PLEGEND01